ESCORT

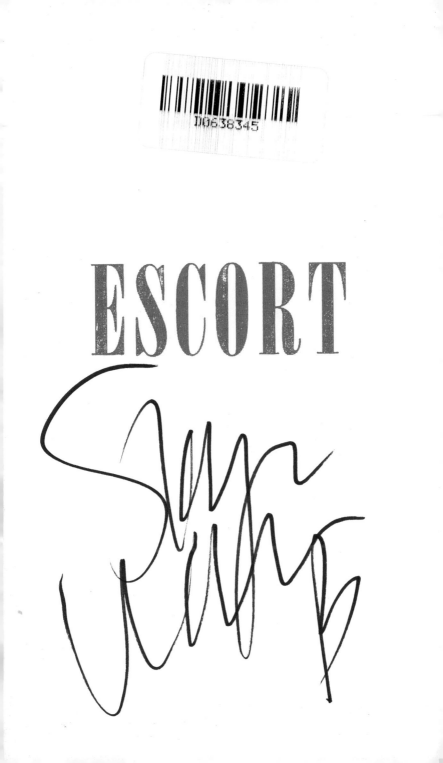

Chapter One

THE CITY LOOKS beautiful at night, its rough edges kissed by moonlight, bright neon lights full of hope. My Bugatti slices through the darkness, smooths over cracked downtown streets. The leather is warm on the steering wheel, the gears smooth under my control. Every muscle in my body hums with anticipation, the certainty that I'm going to get laid tonight. It's more than sex that gets me off. It's the journey. Discovering what makes a woman work. What holds her back and what lets her go.

I pull into the valet driveway and toss my keys to Alejandro, who has three kids at home and another one on the way. "Take care of her," I tell him, slipping a twenty into his palm.

"It's my pleasure," he says, giving the gleaming curves an admiring look.

She's gorgeous, this car. The first thing I purchased for myself once I was done scrabbling for scraps. Once I learned how to use my particular talents. Her form is both sleek and curvy, the kind of body that drives a man to his knees. But it's not the way she looks that I love best. It's the way she moves. The engine that has a mind of her own, sometimes sweet surrender, sometimes temperamental.

I love her best when she gives me a challenge.

L'Etoile is a luxury hotel with 24-karat gold chandeliers and white marble floors. A slice of European aesthetic in the center of Tanglewood's urban sprawl. It's garish and expensive, which suits me fine. It was founded in the forties by a woman who claimed to be French nobility. In reality, she was the madame of a lucrative brothel.

That suits me fine, as well.

The front counter is carved with ornate scrolls and baby angels. A woman stands behind them. Jessica, her name tag says. I give her a winning smile, and her brown eyes widen. "Good evening to you. Is there perhaps a message left for me? Hugo Bellmont."

Her expression becomes soft, vulnerable. I should be very tired of this expression, especially when it comes so easily, but my male pride is a simple creature. It does not mind making women swoon, again and again.

"I… I can check for you." She looks around

for a moment, almost dazed. As if it's never occurred to her that people might come to the desk for messages.

"You have my gratitude."

After some fumbling, her cheeks deeply pink, she locates a stack of envelopes in one of the little cubbies. There is one with black script that I can recognize as my name from here. "Here you are."

I think about what would be required to undress her, to take off her clothes and what remains of her defenses. Very little, but we would both enjoy the journey. Alas, she isn't my intended partner tonight.

Inside the envelope is a hotel key card, which leads to the penthouse.

I've been to a hundred penthouses inside the city. And several outside of it. Each one is its own brand of ridiculous luxury. That's part of the heavy price tag, the ridiculousness. Bathtubs that could fit a baby elephant. Private infinity pools. A helipad complete with exclusive helicopter usage. You don't spring for the penthouse unless you want to be wowed.

Somehow I've never been to the penthouse in L'Etoile.

It's always eluded me. And haunted me.

It isn't the amenities that interest me. A bed

made of solid gold. Draperies spun from a rare Chinese silkworm. Whatever they are I'm sure they're lovely, but it's the person who rents them that I want to meet. My chest feels tight with anticipation. A heavy beat through my veins, because this is more than a client. This is someone who might have access to the current owner of this hotel.

I shouldn't get my hopes up, but hopes aren't under my control. They rise and rise, high enough that I have to turn my thoughts away from revenge. To something much more base. Sex.

There's a private elevator that leads only to the penthouse and the private rooftop gardens. It requires the key card to call it down. There are three buttons on the inside wood panel: L for lobby, P for penthouse, and R for the roof. There's also the silhouette of a bell. I suppose that's for if, in the space between the lobby and their suite, they decide they need champagne and strawberries delivered. I could call down for some. Or I could have brought some flowers. Props, you could say. Props to charm a lady, but I don't need them. Don't want them. I pride myself on making them feel like they're the most incredible woman I've ever met, because for one night they are.

A soft chime signals my arrival. The doors

slide open.

I was prepared for any type of penthouse decor. Something lush and antique to match the lower floors. Something modern and sleek to appeal to the upscale traveler.

What I'm looking at isn't a penthouse at all. Not one I've ever seen.

There's a lumpy corduroy sofa in front of a gilded brick fireplace. A pile of old books about to topple over on a side table that probably came from Ikea. Through the room I can see floor-to-ceiling windows that would have been the focal point, but they've been covered by drapes. That alone would not be remarkable, except for the string of star-shaped plastic lights that traipse across them. It takes me a moment to realize that my mouth is open. Shocked. I'm shocked, which is pleasant enough considering it's a novelty. How long has it been since something surprised me? And where is the object of that surprise? There is no woman to greet me. No seductress. No glamourous woman ready for the night of her life. God, what is that strange tightening in my chest? It feels like anticipation, deep and true, and it's been a lifetime since I felt that.

"Hello," I call, stepping into the suite.

There's a thump from the bedroom. A woman

pops her head around the corner, all frizzy hair and wild eyes and plump pink lips. She wears a black dress with a startlingly high neck, lace on top, the kind that a matron would wear—but her skin is perfectly smooth, her eyes wide. This is a young woman. Younger than myself, her clothes an anachronism.

Her expression? Pure relief. "Oh thank God."

She sounds so sincere that I have visions of an orgasm emergency. A deficiency so intense she had to dial a twenty-four-hour line to have it fixed. There's something undeniably hot about the idea of a woman in dire straits and me the only one who can help.

"Hugo Bellmont," I tell her, providing a small bow. "At your service."

And then I give her the smile. Not the megawatt one that I used downstairs. I give her the slow, suggestive one that lets her know every dirty thing that I'm thinking.

It isn't fake. It doesn't need to be. Not with her whispery curls that I'd love to feel in my fist. Not with the pale freckles across her nose that I'd love to track all the way down her body.

Her eyes are an interesting pale green. I want to look into them while I go down on her.

Every single dirty thought is in the smallest

smile.

Except she disappears back into the bedroom. "In here!"

How unusual. I've never met a woman as hurried about her sexual requirements. She sounds worried, almost frantic, and I haven't even been here sixty seconds.

I follow her, feeling for the first time in years out of my depth. It's a nice feeling, a pleasant simmer in my veins. My steps feel lighter across the plush carpet.

At the threshold I barely have time to register the strange furniture. It's large and antique. Expensive but mismatched. As if they crammed an estate sale into one room.

The young woman is bent over a large dresser, her ass perfectly plump. I could fill my hands with her. Could press my new erection against the crease. Except it isn't a sexy pose.

Instead she seems to be looking *behind* the dresser.

"It's okay," she's saying, breathless. "Come out, sweetie. You can do it."

Based on the sweet tone of her voice and the cat dish I spotted on the way inside, I already know what I'm going to see when I peek over the top of the dresser. Sure enough, there's a fluffy cat with bright yellow eyes peering up at me.

I don't have much experience with cats. They were one level up from rodents where I grew up, useful for catching rats and underfoot in dark alleys.

However, my experience with pussies of a different sort translates just fine, because I can see exactly what's happened to the poor girl. She's backed herself all the way into a corner, made her body so small she can't possibly come out.

No matter how nicely her owner coaxes her, it won't work. It can't possibly. Something like this isn't solved with words; it's solved with a confident, calming touch.

I straighten enough to pull off my jacket. "If you'll allow me."

The woman glances back at me, her eyes going wide as she sees my forearms where I'm rolling up my sleeves. "What are you going to do?"

"I assume you wish me to retrieve the cat."

"Rescue her," she corrects. "Because you have long arms."

I've had women compliment my length before, but usually they're referring to a different body part. Nothing about this night is usual, maybe that's why I like it so much. "Happy to be of service."

"She's very nervous. She might scratch you."

"Wouldn't be the first time." I give her a small smile, and this time I'm rewarded by a pinkening of her cheeks. "Now if you would move aside. I require room to work."

She scoots herself around me, careful not to touch, sucking in her breath as she passes. Is she afraid of me? I don't think so. At least not the ordinary fear a woman might have of a man. Instead she seems wary, much like the cat that watches me from behind the dresser, nervous of the world and its unknowns, terrified of everything and nothing at all.

With both hands braced on the side of the dresser, I use all my strength to lift it. As I suspected, it's an ancient piece, made back when they used solid wood for every beam and joint. It probably weighs a thousand pounds, which is why the woman didn't move it first. I manage to move it two inches farther from the wall, which isn't enough for a person to walk behind, but is enough for a cat. This one would wander out eventually, probably when she wants to eat, but I don't think my client will relax until she does.

So I return to the far end of the dresser, near the corner, and bend to look at the cat. She stares at me, her eyes almost glowing, unfathomable.

"You're a beauty, aren't you?" I murmur.

No response. She doesn't even blink.

"I could talk to you for hours," I say, reaching down to stroke the top of her head.

She's soft and unexpectedly fragile beneath all that fur. It's almost like armor, the thickness of it. It makes her seem larger than she is. "I could talk for hours, and you still wouldn't trust me, would you? You won't believe a thing I say, so I'll just have to show you."

I don't change the cadence of my voice, not even as I reach below the cat and scoop her up, not even as I clasp her securely against my chest and pet her head. She curls against me with a faint purr of relief, her thick tail swishing back and forth in gratitude.

"Oh my God, thank you," the woman says, looking torn between snatching her cat away and coming near me. Quite a dilemma, she has. "She's never been back there, but I startled her, and then she wouldn't come out." She stops herself, flushing. "Sorry, I babble when I'm nervous."

And it's adorable, but I know better than to tell her that.

"My assistance does come with a price," I say instead.

Her eyes widen. "What?"

"Your name. It's only fair now that I'm holding your pussy."

Ah, the color of her cheeks. They remind me of sunsets with wind from the west, the kind that herald good weather for sailors the following day. "Bee," she says.

"The kind that make honey?"

"No, Bea like Beatrix." She makes a face. "It was my grandmother's name."

I would love to say a name as unique as Beatrix while I pound into her, but it's clear she'd rather I called her by the nickname. Anyway, it suits her. Simple on the surface, a thousand meanings beneath. "It's a pleasure to meet you, Bea. And your cat," I prompt.

"Minette," she answers, her expression softening.

Upon hearing her name, the cat seems to realize she's been far too content in a stranger's arms. She pulls herself back, a little haughty, and leaps onto the floor. Only then, from the relative safety of two feet, does she turn back to give me a warning hiss.

Then she swishes away with a walk I can only admire.

"I suppose I haven't made a friend," I say ruefully.

Bea grins. "Are you kidding? She didn't take a swipe at you. I'm pretty sure that means she loves you in Minette language. She doesn't like new people."

Why do you travel with a cat who dislikes new people? I suppose she could keep her locked up in penthouse suites around the country, wealthy enough to insist that her cat sit with her in first class instead of locked in steerage, but it still seems like a strange pet to travel with.

Come to think of it, the pet isn't the only thing strange. The old furniture. The young woman who's looking at me with a mixture of trepidation and hope.

"Is it possible…" I say, almost reluctant to ask, but needing to know. "That she doesn't meet a lot of people because she *lives* on the top floor of an exclusive boutique hotel?"

Green eyes blink at me, as wide as the ones that looked at me from behind the dresser. As if I've trapped her there. As if I'm the only one who can get her out. "Ah. Yes." She laughs a little. "What gave it away?"

A million things, but mostly the fact that Bea looks so skittish I think I could spook her if I move too fast. I nod toward a painting on the wall, which features a smaller version of Minette in pointillism. "I assume it's not standard concierge service to paint a masterpiece of the guest's pet. Though if it is, you really have to mention that in the Expedia review."

She laughs, the sound light as air, making my chest feel full. "I'm guessing Olivier would rather paint her than clean her litterbox."

So she's on a first-name basis with the concierge. It means she's been living here for a while, most likely, which is interesting because she can't be older than twenty. The high-necked dress is strange for someone that young, but it's surprisingly sexy. It conforms to her figure, emphasizing her curves and making my blood run hot.

Her smile fades. "It's not a problem, is it? Me living here?"

As quickly as that, my profession fills the air like smoke. Like a bomb went off.

"It's no problem," I assure her. The agency will send me to a hotel room as easily as a client's high-rise condo. There's no difference as long as the credit card charge goes through.

She bites her lip, looking anywhere except the large antique bed. "Do you... I mean, did you want to just *start* or..."

"Perhaps let's go into the living room," I tell her, already leading the way, my hand light on her lower back. This is the way I picked up the cat, moving her before she really had to think about it, saving her from herself. "I would love to talk to you first."

And find out why this beautiful and nervous young woman hired an escort.

CHAPTER TWO

THERE ARE ASS men and there are breast men. I can appreciate a beautiful ass or a nice rack. The blood in my veins is red, after all. But what I really am, what drives me absolutely crazy, what seems obscene even though women walk around with them in full view, are freckles. There's something about them, the way they scatter over skin, the knowledge of the other places they must cover, that makes me hard as a rock. I have this primal instinct to map the constellations on Bea's body.

Her black dress covers more than it shows. The fabric reveals an hourglass figure that I would love to run my hands along, but we aren't close to that. And above the high neckline, that's where the freckles begin. Only a shade darker than her natural skin color, which is pale.

Pale enough to turn a charming pink whenever she's nervous.

"Thank you for coming," she says, pink all the

way from the point of her nose to her neck. I would bet tonight's entire fee, which is sizable, that the pink extends across her breasts.

Everything about her is closed, her legs pressed together where she perches on the armchair, her lips clamped shut as if to keep herself from saying more. In contrast I'm a study in openness, my ankle slung over my knee, arm stretched across the top of the sofa.

"It's my pleasure," I assure her. "I'm touched that you trust me in your home."

She glances around as if considering for the first time that she ought not have invited me inside. "We could get a room downstairs, maybe. Unless they're sold out."

"I'd rather be where you're most comfortable."

She gives a small laugh of embarrassment. "I'm not sure I'm capable of being comfortable."

"Shall we call down for dinner?" I offer, mostly because the opportunity to eat and drink and breathe will help soothe her. But also because it will give me more time with her, this woman who may hold the answers to my long-held questions.

"No, thank you."

"We could go out. I know a lovely bistro not two blocks away."

She shakes her head, almost stricken. "No."

Such refusal, this one has. Such determination.

Her eyes are wary, watching as I stroke the brocade fabric of the sofa leisurely. It's almost like she expects me to lunge at her, to rip her clothes away without any discussion. Of course I would most enjoy that, if I thought she wanted me to do it.

My curiosity is a living, breathing presence in the room. I want to unravel her secrets. Why does the idea of leaving make her anxiety spike like a tangible blaze in the air?

I decide to go for frankness. "You're a lovely woman, Bea. It would be an honor to spend the evening with you, but I have to be honest. I don't usually work for clients as young as you."

A blink. "You don't?"

One shoulder lifts. "The CEO of a multinational corporation who realizes she's spent more time on work than building a social life. A divorcee who wants to experience pleasure without resentment. They are the usual, but I have a feeling those don't quite apply to you."

"Not exactly," she says, cheeks almost cherry pink.

The cat has found a perch on top of an old

rolltop desk, her yellow eyes trained on me. I don't mind one female looking at me. Don't mind two. To be honest I have a bit of the exhibitionist in me, one of the many reasons I'm in the perfect profession. I know without looking that my shoes are perfectly shined, my bespoke suit conforming effortlessly to my body. Bea's green gaze, both nervous and curious, is the best foreplay I could want.

"I don't need to know what led you to call me, certainly not the details of your circumstances, but it would help if I knew what you expect out of our evening."

"Oh God," she says on a groan. "I'm screwing this up, aren't I? There's probably a secret handshake or something and I don't know it. You must think I'm insane."

I shake my head, slow and slight. "No secret handshake, I promise. There's only you and me, having a conversation about pleasure."

The word seems to take her aback. "Pleasure?"

"That's the nature of my business, yes." My body tightens, because it would be pleasure indeed to touch this woman. To kiss her. To make her moan for me.

Although I might have to rethink that plan, because the word *pleasure* might as well have been *medieval torture* based on the way Bea looks at me. "I thought we were going to have sex."

She sounds so forlorn it could break my heart.

Instead I laugh, a small huff of breath, because I can't afford to have a heart.

"Sex," I say, standing to full height, circling the scuffed oriental coffee table, standing behind her chair. "And pleasure. Pleasure and sex. They're interchangeable."

I brush my knuckles over the side of her neck, a demonstration. Her wild curls tickle my skin.

It's provocative, this. If she had agreed to dinner, I would have started with small touches— a glance of my palm against the small of her back as I pulled out her chair, holding her hand while we talked over a glass of wine. Perhaps being so bold as to run a finger along the inside of hers, where it's more sensitive. She would shiver; her gaze would meet mine.

There's an order to these things. You can move fast or slow, but there's still an order.

"We can skip the pleasure part," she says, her voice high, her breathing faster. Her chest rises and falls in the black dress, made all the more alluring by how much it covers. She's a mystery. The black sky in the city. I have to work to see her secrets.

"No," I chide gently. "We focus on the pleasure. That's the point."

"What if—" Her breath catches as I drop the back of my hand over her collarbone, a reverse caress. That's what one does for a skittish creature like her. "What if I have a different point?"

"And what point would that be, my sweet Bea?"

"I want to lose my virginity," she says, so fast it comes out as a single word.

IWANTTOLOSEMYVIRGINITY. It takes my lust-warmed brain a full minute to comprehend. She's not only nervous, this woman. She's a virgin.

My hand freezes. I yank it away. "Pardon me?"

I can't have heard her correctly. There is no chance in hell that this beautiful young woman, as strange and interesting as she is, is a virgin. No chance in hell that I was the one tasked to be her first. I could not possibly spread her legs and thrust inside her, knowing that no one's ever been there. It would be a physical impossibility. Never. No possible way.

"It doesn't have to take long," she says, suddenly earnest. Almost begging me. "I don't need...you know...whatever you do for other women. I only want the sex."

My God. "You *are* insane."

A scrunch of her nose. "Well, you don't have to sound too surprised. It is what I requested when I called. The woman said that's what you do."

"I'm not taking your virginity." On some level I might have guessed this about her. If I had considered it even possible, I might have. Virgins don't hire me. They stammer and giggle and turn away from me, their protective instincts strong enough to send them in the opposite direction. So perhaps I can be forgiven for not recognizing this one, so forthright.

Bea frowns. "Is that a different department or something?"

She's mocking me. She's mocking me for being, well, prudish, and I feel strangely buoyant. I could float away with the absurdity of it. "Yes, it's a different department. The department of a frat boy who fumbles around in the dark."

"Are you seriously not going to do it?"

The irony is enough to flatten me, that this is a woman I might have pursued outside this job. She would have been too young for me, even if I weren't an escort and she wasn't my client. That wouldn't have stopped me from wanting her.

But in another incarnation, if I had been one of those fumbling frat boys, I would have followed this woman to the ends of the earth. That's a hypothetical scenario on multiple levels, but I'm good at hypotheticals, which is another reason I'm good at my job.

So good that I please every single client I've ever had.

Until this one, apparently.

"I'm seriously not going to do it."

A small line forms between her eyes. "Is it because I'm, you know. Not pretty enough?"

There are about a thousand ways that I'm beneath the woman in front of me. The fact that she might think I'm turning her down makes me want to flay my skin off.

Well, technically I am turning her down. "It's for your own good."

And then she makes a sound. Kind of like *ugh* but more annoyed.

"Look, I don't know what made you call to the agency, what made you think your first time should be a transaction instead of a meaningful experience, but I will not help you do it."

"Is this because I said no pleasure?"

I glare at her. "You must insist on pleasure. Regardless of who you're with."

"From a fumbling frat boy?" She sounds dubious. "It seems to me that if you were really concerned with making my first time pleasurable, you would be the one to do it."

There's only one thing I find sexier than freckles, and it's a sharp wit. I am ready to get on my knees for this woman, even as I know I should walk away. In short, I am screwed.

CHAPTER THREE

THIS IS HOW we end up at the hotel restaurant downstairs. I offered to take her out, would have preferred it, after the strangeness of our meeting. To text a friend of mine at the hottest restaurant in Tanglewood and secure a table for us.

It would have given me a sense of normalcy. Most of the women I see prefer to be courted before I take them to bed. And I enjoy courting them.

Beau Ciel has, predictably, a pretentious maître d'. Less predictably, Bea greets him with the smile of an old friend. "I'm sorry I didn't make reservations, Pierre."

Of course not, he tells her. *She needn't ever*, he tells her.

Then we are led to a private table, tucked behind heavy velvet curtains. The ceiling has been painted with a thousand stars on a dark background. It feels like looking up in a dream.

"You come here often?" I ask, keeping my voice casual.

She studies the menu like it holds the answer if she can only find it. I would bet that she knows every single item listed there. That she's tried them all. "Mostly by room service. I don't usually come down."

I warn myself not to ask how long she's lived in the hotel. It's too personal of a question, even for two individuals who are going to have sex. The only purpose would be to assuage my curiosity. It would not set her at ease. It would not seduce her. I must not ask.

"How long have you lived in L'Etoile?"

Damn.

The words are out before I can even comprehend them. I have only ever been charming with women. It is my one skill in life, discovered before I knew what I was doing, honed over the years. How has this one slip of a woman reduced me to a bumbling first date?

A faint flush touches her cheeks.

"You don't have to answer," I tell her because she shouldn't answer.

"Twelve years," she says so softly I barely hear it. Then her eyes meet mine, the soft green of them like a fog I don't want to clear. "That's weird, isn't it?"

It's very, very weird. "Of course not. You must love it here."

She lifts one slender shoulder in a shrug. "It's safe," she says.

I swallow down every other question that comes to mind. She can't be much older than twenty. Twenty-one, perhaps. Twelve years means she's lived here since she was a child. There was no sign of a parent in that hotel suite. So who raised her there?

An image flashes through my mind, of the princess locked in a tower, her hair dropped out of the window for a prince to climb up. I have always been dramatic, mind. This isn't anything new. *Un rêveur*, my mother called me. Anyway, this girl could never be the princess from the story. Her hair is a wild mass of curls, completely unsuitable for climbing rope.

"Where do *you* live?" she asks, a challenge in her voice.

I understand that she's turning the tables, attempting to make me feel uncomfortable the way that she is uncomfortable. There is nothing personal about my living space, however. "A loft in a recent development on the east side. Beige carpet. Granite counters. It is also safe."

Her lips twist as if she's fighting a smile. "That sounds very…"

"Boring?"

"I was going to say normal."

I lean back in the chair, crossing one ankle over my knee. This is a conversation I'm comfortable with. The woman's curiosity about the life of a high-priced male escort. It doesn't bother me. It isn't even about me. They aren't asking about Hugo Bellmont, the man. They want the persona. That's all I have to give them, anyway.

"Did you expect me to have shag carpets and a mirror on the ceiling?"

She pauses as if fighting with herself. In the end her curiosity must get the better of her because she blurts out, "Why would you have a mirror on the ceiling?"

"To watch you," I tell her, my voice low and blunt. "While you ride me. To see your beautiful ass move as you make yourself come. To turn you over so that you can see mine."

Her mouth is open, eyes wide. I've shocked her. "Oh."

"But we aren't going to have sex in my boring loft with its boring walls. After we've eaten and enjoyed each other's company, I'm going to ask you to take me upstairs."

She makes a sound, like a squeak. I want her to make it again when I'm inside her.

"And you will say yes, Bea, won't you?"

"Maybe not," she says, but it's a thin rebellion. I can hear the arousal in her voice.

"You will, because you were curious about the pleasure. You didn't want it, which is interesting. Maybe sex without orgasms seems to you like your penthouse—safe. But I won't be safe, sweetheart. I will make you come so hard you cannot breathe."

Her pretty breasts rise and fall under the black dress. "That is—that is—"

Before she can tell me what that is, the waiter arrives. He unveils an expensive Bordeaux, which is on the house. I order the steak au poivre, medium rare, to give her time to get her bearings. She does not even glance at the menu as she orders for herself a blanquette de veau, in an accent more Parisian than my own. Interesting.

When the waiter takes our menus away, I busy myself with my cuff link. I have learned the art of foreplay, which extends outside of the bedroom. It starts right now, when I make her feel something only to retreat. The absence makes it sweeter.

Except she takes me by surprise. "Hugo," she

says, almost tasting the name.

I look up at her, this fairy creature, at her wildfire hair and sea-moss eyes. Her smile is all the more devastating because it's pointed at herself.

"You aren't even hungry, are you?"

My eyebrows go up. That isn't what I expected her to say. "Hungry? No. But I'm always willing to eat, especially food that is delicious and rare."

We aren't talking about food. "Don't you ever get tired of it?" she asks.

"Well, if you hadn't already told me, I would know now that you haven't had sex by the question alone. At least not good sex. If you had, you would know the answer to that. We could eat all night, and I would never tire."

CHAPTER FOUR

IT'S WHEN WE get to the crème brûlée that I realize something has changed. The conversation is still foreplay, but we aren't talking about sex. Even in veiled terms. We're talking about childhood and dreams. We're talking about intimacy, which is all the more disturbing.

"It's the cars," I admit my weakness. "I would see them pull up night after night with rich men and beautiful women. These Porches and Bugattis. I knew that one day that would be me."

"And now that *is* you," she says, pride in her voice, as if anyone would consider being a prostitute a success.

"I suppose—" Suspicion narrows my eyes. "How do you know what I drive?"

She flushes a deep crimson. "I may have seen you out the window."

"Really?" I ask, because it's the right thing to say. It makes her feel charmed, but the truth is, I'm the one charmed by her. This sweet, mysterious creature.

"I don't usually use that window," she says, the words rushing together. "It's too bright from the lights on that street unless I keep the drapes shut. But this time... well, I was over there."

"And?" I prod gently because there's clearly more.

"And there was so much dust. I sneezed, and then the lamp fell over, and then Minette got so freaked out she ran behind the dresser and wouldn't come out."

I don't mean to laugh, but the image of this girl watching for me out the window like a nervous prom date is too adorable. "I'm sorry," I tell the hands that are hiding her face. "I'm really not laughing at you."

"I think you are," she says, her voice muffled.

"Bea. Bea, look at me."

Her hands finally drop, revealing this wry twist on her lips that I'm coming to recognize. "Are you done now?"

"Only getting started, darling. But I do have to ask, why do you live here? Besides the fact that it's safe. You must have money to go anywhere."

At some point in the meal there was a bottle of wine. It hasn't made me drunk, but there is a pleasant lightness to me. Any walls I might have had are gone.

The same might be true for Bea, because she leans close as if to tell me a secret. "Because I don't leave. I can't."

"Don't leave where?"

"L'Etoile."

"You mean you aren't allowed to move?" I understand what she's telling me, but I don't want to understand. This woman is so young, so full of life. How can she be imprisoned?

"No, I mean I don't leave the hotel. Like, to go to the grocery store. Or the park. Or anywhere."

Jesus. "How long has it been since you left? I mean, you weren't born here, were you?"

"No, I wasn't born here. I moved in when I was ten. I was... troubled, you know? The way only a rich kid can be." She laughs at herself, the sound hollow. "So my guardian, he got me a tutor who came every day. A therapist who came every week, for all the good that did."

I blow out a breath. So many years in the tower. "That's terrible."

She makes a face, self-deprecating. "Yes, it's a hard life, living in the penthouse."

"'I am a winged creature who is too rarely allowed to use its wings.'"

With a strange look she replies, "'Ecstasies do not occur often enough.'"

"So you can quote the *Diary of Anais Nin*, but you do not believe in pleasure?"

"It's not that I don't believe in pleasure," she says, her voice painfully earnest. "I'm sure it's very nice. But it isn't necessary tonight. Only the act itself."

"The act?" I'm taunting her, and it's only a little about foreplay.

"Fine," she says, speaking fast like she does when she's nervous. "Fine. I want to have sex with you. I want you to have sex with me. You know, the whole thing."

There's more she isn't telling me, and it feels important. I have never asked a woman her motives for hiring me before. It's never mattered. "Because you can't leave?"

"Yes, because I want to do this thing, and I need to do it *here*."

I glance behind her, at the many meals happening beyond the hanging curtain. There are women who look at me. And men. I am somewhat ostentatious with my suit and my assuredness. But even beside me, she shines. "And there has never been a man passing through the hotel that you have wanted? Someone sitting at the bar who bought you a drink?"

"There's you," she says softly, which isn't really an answer.

It's a distraction, and a successful one. Because for the first time in a long time, maybe ever, I want her. Not her body or her money. I want to unlock her secrets. "Then let's go upstairs, and we will see if we can make those ecstasies come more often."

CHAPTER FIVE

ENTERING THE PENTHOUSE, this time knowing that Bea lives here, is a revelation. Minette greets us with a plaintive meow, winding around our ankles as if we both belong.

There is a coat rack beside the entrance, draped with a herringbone coat. A tightly wrapped umbrella sits in the base. I know without touching them that they won't be damp, despite the weather, because Bea didn't go outside today. She didn't go outside yesterday. How long has it been since she stepped foot outside this hotel?

"Do you want some coffee?" she asks in that too-fast way. I'm not sure whether she's asking as a kind of date etiquette or whether she wants a reprieve, but I say what I always tell my clients.

"Yes, please. I would love some."

I follow her to the corner of the suite where a wet bar would be. It's been expanded, I see, to include a small two-range stove top with a wardrobe beside it that I assume serves as a pantry. It's still less than even a small apartment would offer, but much more utility than any ordinary penthouse suite. A gleaming mini-fridge must hold the meager contents of her food supply, when she doesn't order down for baked camembert or oysters.

What a life she leads, both decadent and desolate.

Her hands are shaking. The mug trembles for a beat too long against the metal plate of the fancy machinery, revealing her weakness. I take it from her gently, setting it aside.

"Darling," I say softly.

She gives a small shudder. It isn't quite a sob. That's the only warning I have before she crumples, not against anything, not on top of anything, it's more like she becomes suddenly small. Tiny. Like she's shoved herself behind a dresser in an effort to be invisible.

I wrap her in my arms before I can think better of it. That's what I'm here for, isn't it? To provide comfort with my body. That's all I am— my hands or my mouth. My cock. And if that makes me feel cold and paper-thin, it does not matter.

This woman, though, she seems to like me for my arms.

I stroke her back softly, murmuring words of assurance. In French, I realize belatedly, but it doesn't matter. She proved downstairs she could understand, and the language doesn't matter. Not for what we're doing here.

Her body feels impossibly slight in my grasp, like smoke that will disappear if I hold too hard. But her hair—God, her hair. It does not care that she is trying to make herself small; it's a perfect bronze cloud, tickling my nose, curling gently into my skin.

Her shoulders shake against me. The sound of her worry and her grief carve themselves into my skin, leaving marks I'm not sure will be gone by morning.

"Bea." I tilt her tear-stained face up with my thumb and forefinger. "Tell me what's wrong. Why have you called me here tonight? Why are you hurting?"

"I'm embarrassed," she says, her cheeks a deep red. "I mean, I know I should have gone downstairs to the bar. That makes way more sense than paying someone to have sex with me."

"Why didn't you?" I'm genuinely curious.

She speaks into my chest, her voice muffled. "I did. Five nights in a row, I wore this dress and went downstairs. Every night someone would send me a drink."

My voice is softer now. "Did you accept?"

"I tried to. I took a sip and gave them a smile when they sat down at the stool next to me. But it was too real somehow. Like they would expect something more than... you know."

"Sex," I say with gentle encouragement.

"Sex," she repeats.

The word sends a soft breath of heat into my cock. God, this woman. Even hearing her say the word is enough to make me hard. What will it feel like to peel the black dress from her body? To hear her moans and sighs and a thousand other sounds?

"I have no expectation," I tell her. "Not even sex. If you want to sit with me and recite nursery rhymes, that is what we'll do. Or if you'd like me to leave. However..."

She looks at me, hope in her green eyes. "However?"

"However, it would be an honor to take you to bed tonight."

"Even though I haven't done it before?"

Especially because of that.

So much that it terrified me before, when she first told me. But I've had time to consider it over dinner, and besides the caveman-like effect it has on my body, how hard she makes me, it makes sense that I should be the one to do this.

One of those assholes at the bar, what if they don't make her come? What if they demand more from her than she wants to give? No, the way to make this good for her is to do it myself.

Even though I haven't done it before?

"Even though," I tell her, my voice grave.

She smiles, then, the parting of clouds. "My friend Harper said this would be a thousand times more awkward than a one-night stand, but it's not. It's easier. Is that wrong?"

"It's perfectly right."

I said it to reassure her, but I'm the one reassured when I stroke my thumb across her cheek. It feels perfectly right to bend my head and breathe in the faint smell of lavender. Perfectly right to press my mouth against her plush lips.

She opens her mouth with an acquiescent sigh, and I know she's still finding this easier. The men downstairs, none of them could have given her this. There's seduction in my movements, but confidence too. The kind of confidence that can only come from knowing I can please her.

An entire city of men who would have had her, who would have been happy for the privilege of a single night, no money exchanging hands, and she paid for me.

I wasn't lying to her before. It will be an honor.

CHAPTER SIX

HER FRECKLES DON'T taste like anything. I know that, but I can't stop kissing them. Can't stop following the reckless trail across her cheek and below her jaw. I swear there's stardust in them, something elemental and bright. They singe my lips, my tongue.

She makes a sound of surprise, a strangled little gasp in her throat. "Is this regular? I thought it would be more like…"

"More like what?" I don't pause to give her time to answer. She must find the wherewithal even while I move my body closer to hers. Her hands flutter against my shoulders, not pushing me away, not pulling me close. They are confused, those hands.

"Like the movies."

That makes me stop. I pull back so I can look into her pale green eyes. Jade, I realize. They're the color of jade, the kind of stone you would hang on a gold chain. "What movies?"

This level of red, it's an emergency. Her cheeks burn. "You know."

"Do you watch porn, darling?"

"Only for instructional purposes," she says too fast.

I do not laugh. I think I should get a medal for not laughing at this. "And what did you learn from the porn movies you watched?" I ask, quite seriously.

"Usually they…you know. The clothes come off."

Naturally I am desperate to know what sort of clothes came off. Was there a nurse's uniform? Or perhaps a man dressed as a burglar, come to tie her up? "Do you want to take off your clothes?"

"No," she says on a squeak.

Of course not. Because she isn't ready for that, despite the dubious education porn movies have given her. She's practically vibrating with nervousness. "Then you'll keep your clothes on. For now. For as long as you want them. You're safe with me."

Her eyes focus with puzzlement. "Safe?"

It's the reason she stays in this tower, this princess with red hair. Because it's safe. And that's what I must be, if I'm to be allowed to stay. "Safe," I say. "Tell me what you're thinking."

She looks reluctant, biting her lip.

"No matter what you say, I won't be angry. Cross my heart."

"I'm worried you aren't really aroused," she says, fast. "That you're faking it."

It's not the first time a woman has ever worried about that with me, but it *is* the first time I've been as desperate to get a woman naked. That she doubts me now is a great irony. "What makes you think that?"

"In the movies they always show the—the—"

"You don't think my cock is hard?"

She flushes. "I mean, it doesn't have to be."

Now I can't help but laugh. A full belly laugh. When is the last time I had one of these? There are tears at the corner of my eyes. I turn her around, making her face the small countertop with its fancy espresso maker. She's right up against it, her tummy pressed to the curved stone ledge. Then I cover her with my body, my throbbing cock between her sweet ass cheeks, the only barriers her clothes and mine.

She stiffens with a small gasp. "That is—"

"Do you see what you do to it? You make it hard. So hard it hurts."

"I'm sorry."

"No, no," I murmur. "Never apologize for

that. It's all a man can dream of, a woman making him so hard it hurts. Only letting him touch her over her clothes. Dying for a glimpse of bare skin."

She moans a little. "This isn't like the movies."

I press my lips to the small patch behind her ear. "No, it's not like the movies. This is real life, and that's why you called for me, isn't it? Because the movies were not real."

"Yes," she agrees, breathless.

"When the women come, and they squeal and shake, it isn't real. It isn't right. You know that, don't you? They fake it. You won't fake anything, darling." I turn her to face me, because for the first time this is the right way. The only way.

"What if I don't—"

"You will," I assure her, which only seems to worry her more.

A shudder runs through her delicate frame, making her hair vibrate like dewdrops on a flower petal. It only *looks* fragile; in truth it can withstand this earthquake. "It would be easier if it didn't feel so good," she says, her voice plaintive and pleasure-dipped.

"One day you'll tell me why you want sex so badly, without feeling anything."

"I won't," she says, but she's only cross with me because I'm rubbing gentle circles on her back, because it feels so damn good. She arches into my touch, the same way her cat would.

And then I move my hand lower, to the upper curve of her ass. It's a beautiful ass, which is saying something. I've seen more than my fair share. Enjoyed every single one of them, but the picture of her heart-shaped behind, from when she bent over the dresser, is emblazoned in my mind. So perfectly wrapped in black, silky fabric, thick enough to ward most men away. I'm not most men. The challenge only makes it sweeter as I stroke the slope of her, as I feel her gasp in response. I'm the first man to ever traverse this land, something I hadn't thought to find pleasure in. What a barbarian I am. A Viking, to find such deviant delight in taking a young woman's virginity. It has nothing to do with seduction, the palm I place on her, the squeeze I give her. That's pure indulgence on my part, knowing I am the first.

She shifts closer to me, making tiny sounds I'm not sure she hears. Her body is out of her control; it's in mine now. "I don't even know your favorite color," she whispers.

I laugh softly. "Red."

The color of my Bugatti.

"Mine's blue," she says, but she doesn't explain why.

I reach down to the lace hem of her dress, pulling the fabric into careless bunches, until I touch bare skin. It's a godsend, the satin of her. Like opening my mouth to the sky after years of thirst. With a firm grasp I hitch her leg up to my hip, spreading her. "Any other questions?"

Her eyes are hazy. I can see the struggle behind the green curtain, the valiant attempt to string words together as her body comes apart. "Favorite food."

"A tagine," I tell her, not adding that it's my mother's I dream about. The spice of it on a hot night, making me sweat in the dark. This isn't about revealing secrets, not truly. It's about making her feel like she knows me. I won't lie to her, but I won't rip apart my skin to set her at ease either.

That clears enough of the arousal from her eyes to ask, "A tagine?"

It makes me wonder what other foods she hasn't yet experienced, trapped in this gilded prison of hers. Even the richest of foods can be punishment if they're all she can eat. "A stew. Spicy. Do you like spicy food?"

"I don't know," she says, confirming my worst fears.

I want to book us a flight to Thailand or South Africa, to show her a thousand buildings and give her a million new tastes. Like most penthouse suites, this one is large—for a visit, not for a lifetime. "What's your favorite food, darling?"

She pulls back, looking me right in the eyes, proving that though she is untried, she is far from naive. "I haven't found it yet."

Her words travel straight to my groin, a challenge I'm desperate to accept. "You think these questions make it easier? We could talk for hours and hours, darling. And still you would be nervous."

"Then how do people do this?"

I grasp her small hand and place it flat on my chest. "These are your questions. So what do you wish to know?"

Awareness sparks in her eyes. She moves her hand in the smallest circle, testing, asking about the solidity of my body, wondering at the reality of this encounter. I can't let so eager a question go unanswered; I bend my head to capture her lips.

Her other hand flutters against my shoulder before settling there. A butterfly I must be careful not to spook if I want to enjoy its beauty. I dart my tongue against her lips, letting her think about the presence of it before delving into her mouth.

She startles for a moment, and I think, this is it. This was all I'll have of her, this taste. It's shocking, the depth of my disappointment. I can walk away from any woman. We enjoy our time together. And then we part. I have never wanted more, never needed another taste like I do now.

She moans in sweet acquiescence.

I'm overcome with relief I don't want to examine, and I slide my tongue against hers in quiet insistence. The physical sensations are a tidal wave; they drown out any thoughts or worries. They sweep over the both of us, making her breath come faster. She's excited and hungry and needy, and so I can push aside the realization that I am, too.

If my response to her is stronger than I expected, so be it. I can use it to be a better tutor for her. Because that's what I am right now, as experienced as I am, with a virgin—her teacher.

I press my forefinger to the small furrow between her eyes. "You are thinking too hard. Feel, instead." To illustrate my point, I bite her plump bottom lip. It's only a small nip, but enough to make her jump. "Only feel."

Her eyes spark with a lovely rebellion. "Like this?"

I know what she's going to do before she leans forward, before her white teeth peek from between peach-colored lips. There are one, two, three seconds when I could jerk out of reach. And it wouldn't be awkward; I would be too charming for that. I would laugh and cajole and coax her into the most pleasure she's ever known.

It would be a beautiful performance, that. Instead I let her get close enough to hurt me, the sharp pain a brilliant counterpoint to the thrum of anticipation in my veins. It's only a pinch, but I have to close my eyes against the raw force of it.

"Yes," I say, and my voice is lower now. My accent thicker. "Like that."

"What else?" she whispers, and a dark current of arousal runs through me at the hope in her voice. It wasn't only me who was jaded, I realize. It was the women. The women who would call me, because they were tired of selfish, cheating men in their lives. I was happy to give them a reprieve from their loneliness, to take a reprieve from my own, but this is different.

Bea is full of hope, like a curved tendril of green splitting the earth in spring. She makes me want to breathe in deep, to stretch my limbs. To watch her rise.

What else? she asked. This is what else, my hand falling down her side to the indent at her waist. And lower, lower. She sucks in a breath, leaving only cool air against my collarbone.

And still lower.

My hand stops in the space below her stomach, well above her mound. A place that isn't on its own sexual, but a place a man would only touch if he's about to have sex.

"You have practice, yes? You touch yourself."

Her lips form a perfect O because of course she has. She isn't experienced, but she is curious. "That's not weird," she says, a little defensive. The voice of one who has to convince herself.

"But no. Very sexy, that's what it is. I would love to see it."

Her cheeks flame. "I couldn't."

"Maybe later," I say, and then I do something a little forward. I give her a wink. That would not be an introductory lesson on flirting, on foreplay, but I find myself out of my depth with this girl. As if I'm desperate to impress her instead of a hired professional with a job to do.

She bites her lip. "Could I watch *you* do that?"

God, the mouth on her. She can't even say the words, but she manages to say them anyway. So much courage and so much fear. My body tightens with the image of her, leaning forward, lips parted, while I pump my cock. I would become desperate, sweating and swearing, but still I would not come, not until she had looked her fill.

"It would be torture," I tell her honestly. "Exquisite."

She studies the top button on my shirt like it's an elaborate puzzle. It would be so easy to open it myself, without even removing my gaze from her. And it's so much sweeter to watch her struggle with herself.

Then she takes a deep breath as if steeling herself.

Her small fingers brush against my chest through linen, uncertain with the stiff fabric. She pushes the button through the hole, tugging the fabric apart no more than a centimeter.

Another button and another.

She opens my shirt down to my navel before spreading it apart.

I glance down, trying to imagine what I look like for her, dark hair and tanned skin. My body is acceptable. I work out enough to keep myself trim, to bulge a few muscles for the clients who like such things, but that is not my strong suit.

There are weight lifters and ballplayers on the payroll for women who prefer men like that. Myself, I am tall and somewhat spare. It is my smile that makes them choose me, not my body, but Bea looks at me with awe.

"Do you like what you see?" I ask, my voice pure gravel.

I expect her to be demure, to shake her head and avert her eyes, what any well-behaved ingenue would do. Instead she meets my gaze with an impish smile. "Feeling insecure, are you?"

My laugh comes out full-bodied. It takes me by surprise. "A man does like to feel wanted."

"I do want you," she says with a candor I've come to admire from her. An eagerness I've already learned to crave. "But I'm not sure I should have you."

"Do you think I'll hurt you?" I don't think that's her worry, but I have to be certain. It would break me if she thought I would force her to do anything she didn't want to. "We can call the service right now. They can send someone else."

"No," she says, a little too loud, turning pink. "No, not that. It's just that I've spent so long here in these four walls. Seeing the same group of people. Doing the same things."

I hear the starvation in her words, the darkness that closes in on her. "You're afraid because I'm new. Because what we're doing is new. So we will only do what you've already done."

"Do you mean watch me…"

"Masturbate? *Oui*, I could watch that. I would gladly, but I would also love to make you come. It would be a feeling you've had before, only with my fingers instead of yours."

She likes that, I see the excitement brighten her eyes. Her fear recedes into the night. "Here?"

I look around at the small bar and the sofa beyond. "Where do you usually do it?"

"In bed."

My hand links with hers, and we go there together. This is the room where I began this journey, the dresser still slightly ajar from the wall. The mismatched furniture at odds with the sleekness of the penthouse suite. The bed neatly made in anticipation of what's to come, white ruffles in neat alignment. The thought of her wet and horny under this spread is enough to dampen a spot of precum on my boxers. Already my cock hurts with how long I've been hard, but I will wait as long as she needs. Forever, if that's what it takes to make her comfortable.

She turns off the lamp, and I let her, but only because she would normally do this in the dark.

There is only the light spilling in from the doorway, barely enough to see her by.

I pull back the bedspread, messing up her ordered work. The sheets are cool beneath my palm, and I smooth them, smooth them, making them warm and ready.

When I turn back to face her, she looks up at me with luminescent eyes.

Every thought of teaching her, of tutoring her, of remaining aloof from her disappears from my head. There's only the need to kiss her and the physical movement to make it happen. Her lips yield under mine, softer now, quicksand, and I'm sinking.

This time when I touch her, she sighs into my mouth, a sound of infinite relief. I give in to my baser impulses and touch her plump ass, knead and mold her, and then it's my turn to sigh in relief. She is everything warm and vibrant in my arms.

I know a move for every situation, practiced and choreographed to maximize her pleasure, but it's clumsy hands that press her back to the bed, that lift her heavy lace dress in pursuit of ecstasy. I slide my palm up the inside of her thigh, and her hips lift, shocked and seeking.

"Spread for me, Bea."

She does, wordless, her eyes wide moons. There is enough mystery there to make me uncertain about my reception, but then I touch her—ah, there. And she's wet for me, drenched and swollen for my cock. It isn't my cock that she'll get though, only the stroke of my forefinger making her cry out.

"Tell me what you feel."

"I feel wild," she whispers. "And so good. And it hurts. Why does it hurt?"

Beautiful. She's goddamn beautiful. "Because your body knows what it needs." I press my thumb in front of her clit, hovering there in the slickness. "Reach for it."

And then she does, lifting her body in a timeless rhythm. She doesn't need my lessons, that much is clear, not the way she writhes in relentless pursuit, pressing her clit against me.

She could come this way, but I want more. Not only for her.

For me.

I slip my finger inside her. God, she's tight. She would be a vise around my cock, and I feel myself flex inside my pants. I have one knee on the bed, the other leg still planted on the floor. I'm bent over one of the most beautiful women I've ever seen, but I'm still fully dressed.

Part of me wants to open my pants and release myself. To slip inside her heat and take what she's already paid for. But something holds me back.

"Please," she whispers.

Then I'm helpless except to kiss her, to thrust my tongue into her mouth with the same steady gait as I slip my finger inside her. And still she fucks her body against my thumb, the friction making her gasp against my lips.

There is no longer a spiral to the top; she's hovering there, trapped in suspended agony.

Afraid, I realize with a terrible dread.

It's the first time I've ever wondered if I might not make a woman come. Her body is with me, but her mind is afraid. I bite her lip once more, and her attention focuses on me. "Nothing will happen to you," I tell her, even though I have no ability to protect her. No right. "I won't let anything happen to you. Let go for me, Bea. Let go."

She comes with a glorious rush of arousal, her body jerking in wild abandon. I pet her clit with firm strokes of my thumb through her orgasm, and then stroke her sex softly as she comes down, pressing kisses over her nose and across her forehead, telling her how beautiful she is, how sweet. My brave girl.

Everything is perfect in this moment. Her body and its response to me. Even the fact that I'm rock-hard and suffering beneath my suit cannot mar this.

Until her gaze snaps to mine, and everything changes.

All the fear rushes back, tenfold. I see it march in like a thousand pinpoints of darkness, blotting out her bright arousal. And then she bursts into tears.

CHAPTER SEVEN

LIKE MOST BOYS in Tangier I ran wild in the streets while my mother worked twelve-hour shifts. I swiped fruit from the backs of donkeys on their way into the market and learned to pick pockets from the men with glittering women. Almost a million people live between the city walls, speaking ten languages as commonly as the national Arabic, but for the poor son of a hotel maid, there was only the dust and the clamor and the dry burn of the sun. It was a rough existence but also a joyful one. I didn't know anything else.

I knew early not to cry. There was no time with the caregiver with ten babies in the other room. And when I was older, there was always another boy to lash out. And so tears dried before they came out, even when my favorite street dog was run over in front of me, her leg twisted away, held to her only by flesh and tendon, part of her belly exposed. She lay whimpering in my arms until I used my pocketknife to end her suffering.

And still I did not cry.

I don't know what to do with the sobbing young woman on the bed.

My throat feels tight. I've made women moan and scream and beg. Never this. "Did I hurt you? Was I too rough? Forgive me, Bea. I never meant to—"

"It wasn't that." She shakes her head, glancing at me with tearstained eyes, pleading. She wants me to understand, but I don't. Somehow my experience is failing me. My charm is failing me. If she wanted me to whisper to her in Italian on the rooftop, I could do that. If she wanted me to lick her pussy until her body went limp, I could do that. What is it she wants from me?

She buries her face in her hands, shoulders shaking, trying to muffle the sounds of her distress. "Just go. I'm okay. You can go."

There is no way that I can leave her like this. For a moment I stand there, helpless, still fully dressed, my arms outstretched as if to hold her, my cock still uselessly hard in my slacks.

There's a hard pit in my stomach that reminds me of that hot afternoon with the dog limp in my arms, frozen, frozen, the horror of knowing I could do nothing to help.

Except this isn't a packed dirt street in

Tangier.

And I'm not a powerless little boy.

I lift her body into my arms, hearing her startled gasp, and climb into the bed. With gentle determination I cradle her body in my arms. After a breathless moment she buries her face against my chest. Only then can I breathe fully, knowing she's accepted my comfort, small though it is.

My words are useless now; all I have to offer her is my body. That's all I ever have, really. I rock her slowly, back and forth, holding her tight as her sobs slow and then stop.

"This isn't how you usually finish your dates?" she asks, her voice still thick from tears.

My heart squeezes that she's going for humor, that she's trying to make this more comfortable for me. "We finish with whatever you need."

She shudders her way through a sigh. "I'm sorry."

"Don't apologize to me. It tears a strip of skin from me when you do."

Her eyes meet mine, framed by damp lashes. "That makes me want to apologize more."

From somewhere I find the strength to laugh, a light thing, to let her know this is normal, even though it's not, it's not, it's not. I've never made a woman cry. *I've never been with a virgin before, either.* This was a terrible idea. What made me think I could do this? That because I can make a woman come, her body clench and convulse, that I should be trusted with her first time?

"Hey," she says. "I see you blaming yourself. But it wasn't you."

"I'm sure you cry also when room service arrives."

She gives a huff of laughter. "No, I'm sure that would freak Rene out."

"Consider me freaked out," I tell her even though I'm relieved. Thirty seconds ago, she was bawling her eyes out. But this, a woman in need of laughter and reassurance, I can do.

She bites her lip. "I just didn't expect it to feel good."

"You must tell me where you learned these horrible ideas about sex."

"I mean, I knew about orgasms. I've seen them on movies and read about them in books. And I've given them to myself. But this was completely different. Like all my life I've been seeing water through thick glass, and then one day I dive in."

"It makes you sad, this?"

"Yes," she whispers. "It makes me sad, thinking of all those days I never dipped a toe in.

Because I was too afraid. That's the only reason."

"And you wonder what else you're missing."

"I *know* what else I'm missing, but that doesn't make the fear go away."

"Then what does?"

Her green eyes meet mine, a little fearful, a little wry. "Apparently, you."

CHAPTER EIGHT

"**A**ND YOU JUST left her there?"

The question comes from Sutton Cooper, the roughneck of our little group. The censure in his voice leaves no doubt as to his opinion on the matter. He may be a hard-ass, with a background roping steer and raising hell, but he has a hard line about treating women well.

Even if that only means making her breakfast after a night of no-strings sex.

"She paid for the night," I say blandly.

Christopher leans forward in the leather armchair, his eyes dark. They always see right through me. They see through everything. "Have you ever made a girl cry before?"

"But of course, that's why I'm the highest-paid escort in Tanglewood. Because I say sharp and insulting things that make the women cry."

Blue takes a sip of whatever new beer he's drinking. "Has Hugo been sarcastic before?"

"Only when he's upset," says Christopher, the

bastard.

We're sitting at the Den, like we do almost every week. At the beginning there was only Blue and Sutton and me, starting with a handful of dollars in our pockets, determined to make something of ourselves. The Thieves Club, we called it, only half joking—our own Den of thieves. We weren't planning on robbing any banks, but every dollar we earn means taking one away from someone else.

Sutton runs a hand through his blond curls, the ones that can make any woman swoon. Some of the women in the room glance at him as he does it, the light from the amber fixtures reflecting off the golden strands. He's a veritable angel walking the earth—made hard from his fall.

"She must be something," he says, "for you to get shaken up."

"I'm not shaken up."

"So she wasn't something?" Blue says, crossing one booted foot over his knee. He wears only jeans and T-shirts and dusty black boots, in direct violation of the dress code. He wears enough suits running his security company, he says, when he would much rather be in army fatigues.

"She's beautiful, of course. All women are beautiful."

Christopher raises an eyebrow. "So she's ordinary?"

They're baiting me. I know they're baiting me, and still it works. "*Non.* She is perfection. Delicate and pale and covered in freckles. Everywhere, freckles."

"I do love freckles," Sutton says with a wistful sigh.

"And she has a smart mouth that presents itself at the most surprising times. When I think she will be most scared and cowering, that's when she tells me what's what."

Blue grunts because he enjoys a woman with attitude. "Nice."

"And there's something about her—the strangeness of her staying in that hotel, for one thing. Her past. Her secrets. I want to unwrap them as much as I want to take off her clothes."

"Which is a lot," Christopher observes, his voice dry, but I'm not fooled.

He loves secrets as much as I do, with his neat suits and obsidian eyes. He was the last addition to the Thieves Club, one we never expected. But when he went into business with Sutton, he slid into our group as if there had always been a space waiting for him.

With his cold ambition, there is no one better

suited to join us.

Plus he brings the most excellent brandy.

I take a sip, savoring the spice. "Most likely she won't call again. She will find some handsome traveler in the hotel bar, who will finally convince her to leave the safety of her little nest."

The thought turns the brandy sour in my mouth.

"Or not." Blue turns the amber beer bottle in his thick fingers, studying me. "If you really upset her that much she might be too afraid to try again. You might have fucked her up."

I choke on my next sip and set the crystal down. "Thank you for that."

"She's going to call again," Christopher says, raising his finger for the server. The Den has a full bar, of course, but we can bring our own liquor, especially if we have a special bottle. The brandy he brings for me. Obscure craft brews for Blue. His business partner, Sutton, prefers Patrón.

He drinks only wine himself, the kind that must be purchased at auction.

There is terrible hope inside me at that, because Christopher is usually correct.

"Because she wishes to cry again?"

"This is a woman who has spent her whole life behind bars, essentially. Even if they are bars of her own making. She wants to feel something. That's why she called the first time. It's why she'll call again."

I turn to stare into the fire as the server attends to refilling our drinks. Absolute privacy is assured in the Den, but I still would not speak of Bea in front of a stranger. In fact I do not usually tell the Thieves Club about any of the women I'm with, but she's far from usual.

And of course there's the issue of L'Etoile, but I have no intention of telling anyone about that— not even these men. They don't need to know that I have a darker purpose for wanting to go back to the hotel, to get closer to the woman who lives there.

When we're alone again, I lean forward. "I want to see her again, which is enough to convince me that I shouldn't. I don't have feelings for my clients. I pleasure them; they pleasure me. That's all."

"It's clear this has gone beyond that already," Sutton says. He wears a white business shirt, rumpled from a day's use, the sleeves rolled up. They dress alike, he and Christopher, in their high-rise real estate office, but they could not be more different.

"And I'm worried that if I go again, I'll have

sex with her. Of course I will. But how can I do that, knowing she cried when I only made her come? How do you take someone's virginity?"

"Don't ask me," Blue says.

He's the only one of us in a committed relationship. He loves his wife, who had a very rough childhood. Enough that he didn't take her virginity, even though they met as teenagers. I've met Hannah, and she's impossibly sweet; it's heartbreaking to think of her hurt.

"No idea," Christopher adds, but I happen to know he holds a deep fascination with his stepsister. She's the reason he moved to Tanglewood, though he would not admit that.

Even Sutton puts up his hands. "Who wants that kind of responsibility?"

Mon Dieu.

"I am in very big trouble," I announce softly.

The group drinks in silent agreement.

CHAPTER NINE

THE NEXT SATURDAY night I come prepared. The paper bag in my arms isn't about seducing her, at least not about having sex. I already know she will do that with me, but I want to seduce her in other ways. Her mouth and her mind. Maybe then I will be comfortable taking her body.

She opens the door, and her eyes widen. "What's this?"

"I told you I was bringing dinner," I say, stepping over the threshold and heading into the kitchen.

"I thought you meant takeout from downstairs."

"But no. Tonight I will cook for you my favorite meal." Inside this bag is everything I need: half a chicken that has been marinating overnight and roasted before arriving, vegetables, an onion, garlic. An array of spices from my pantry.

Her brow furrows. "A tagine?"

"You remember?"

She ducks her head and hides a shy smile. "I don't think I'll forget anything about that night."

It's rather uncomfortable, having a boulder sitting on my chest. I remove it by clearing my throat. "You can help me by chopping vegetables, if you'd like."

"Of course," she says, picking up an onion.

I take it away. "No need to make you cry so early in the evening. Start with the cauliflower."

That makes her laugh, and I feel myself relax. I have never cooked with a woman, certainly never a client, but we fall into a pattern of quiet preparation.

"Like this?" she asks, showing me the cherry tomatoes in quarters.

Her technique is clumsy, because this tiny kitchen leaves no room for cooking anything but the essentials. It reminds me of the way she kisses, all eagerness, no finesse. "Perfect," I say. "Keep going."

She flashes me a brief, nervous smile before turning back to work. My stomach feels lighter than it should, almost fluttery, and it takes me a moment to realize what this is: nerves. Dear God. She's turning me into a schoolboy.

It's perhaps with too much gusto that I break

down the chicken, letting the slice of the knife split the strange tension in the air. The meat comes apart under my hands, tender and fragrant.

"Tell me about your day," I say, my tone coaxing. I need to get us back to solid ground. We are shallow and flirty; that's fine. But we will not be nervous. There is nothing more at stake here than a fun night together.

"I played for a while. And then—"

"Played what?"

"Oh." She makes an embarrassed face. "I forgot you didn't know. I'm a pianist."

I have to bite my tongue so I don't ask her to play for me. It's not her job to perform for me. It's mine to perform for *her*. Finished with the chicken, I settle the pieces into the dish and wash my hands in the sink. "That's incredible. You play every day?"

A flush this time. "Yes, most days. It's my job actually, so…"

I pause with my hands under the warm water. It's not hard to believe that she's a concert pianist. She has the wild hair and the dreamy atmosphere. And certainly the wealth that would have afforded her the opportunity to train at a world-renowned music school.

But she does not leave this suite. How does a

concert pianist work from home?

She fills in my questioning silence. "I have a video channel. You know, online."

First, there's shock. I turn off the water. This tentative creature exposes herself online? Perhaps not her body, but music is far more intimate than that. And then there's attraction, the kind that makes me want to watch every video she's ever posted. *Damn.* "That's incredible. Would it make you self-conscious if you showed me one of your videos?"

"No. I mean, yes, but not as much as what we did the other night. When I'm playing, that's when I'm the most comfortable. The most... me."

"After we've eaten," I tell her.

She looks more comfortable just talking about music. "I like this. The cooking thing."

"Here, add the vegetables." I hold the pan for her while she puts in carrots, zucchini, onions. On top of that I add the marinade, where they will simmer together on the stove top before serving. Not a traditional terra-cotta dish, but I had to improvise with her small kitchen, doing most of the cooking at my home. "I cook almost every night. It's soothing."

She peers over my arm at the stew. "Why is it

orange?"

"Paprika is what gives it the color. Turmeric. Cinnamon. Ginger."

Her lips form a circle and it's too much of an invitation, whether she means it or not. I touch my forefinger to her bottom lip, giving her the chance to pull away. Her eyes widen, but she doesn't move. I know without trying it that my skin will taste like spices. Without breaking eye contact, I push my finger inside, rubbing my finger pad along her tongue.

"Coriander," I murmur. "Cumin. Olive oil."

She sucks in a breath, which forms a seal around my finger. The pulling sensation almost brings me to my knees, strong enough, shocking enough that I pull away.

"What do you think?" I ask softly.

Her swallow is an audible surrender. "It's really good."

That makes me laugh, but only a little. "Really good? I'll have to try harder."

"I would die," she says, both solemn and playful in a way I'm learning is unique to her, "if it were any better. I wouldn't be able to handle it."

"Poof," I tell her, more playful than solemn. "You would expire on the spot."

Her smile is tilted. "You would do that to me?"

"I suppose you'll have to wait and see."

There are trolls who live under bridges, according to my mother. She was full of superstitions and stories. They were fun when I was small. They turned darker later. These trolls, they make you answer questions in order to pass. That's what I become during dinner, cajoling and curious.

I want to know everything about her, including when she started to play—she was three when she first read music, but she played from the moment her pianist mother sat her on her knee. She played from a young age, and then... and then there was tragedy. She does not tell me what it is, and I don't ask. That's beyond the scope of what we do here. Sorrow has no place here.

And under no circumstances will I make her cry—again.

"When did you begin your video channel?" The tagine turned out to be exceptional, despite her rather sad stove top that heated unevenly.

"A couple years ago." She takes a bite and closes her eyes, giving this little moan I don't think she knows she's doing. It's completely involuntary, that sound. Completely sexual.

When her eyes open again, she looks a little dazed. "I was going through a dark time. Feeling very alone here, so I posted online, thinking maybe I would find another musician going through the same thing. It went viral on social media, and then I had these followers asking for more."

"You must have exceptional talent."

She looks shy, but of course she does. "There are so many talented musicians out there."

"Then what sets you apart?" I ask, half as a taunt, and half because I truly want to know. I see something incredible in her, something almost too sweet to be borne, but that does not mean the world will see it. In fact, the very opposite is usually true: the more rare and precious a gift, the more easily the world will dismiss it.

A helpless shrug is my only answer.

And then I cannot wait any longer. The tagine is only half-gone, our plates almost empty but ready for second helpings, but I have to see her in her element.

The first thing when I get to the website is a picture of her. It's part of the header graphic, a picture of her with her hair a wild halo, the shadows falling dramatically around her, her eyes closed in ecstasy. *Climax,* my sex-ready mind supplies. That's how she will look during climax.

Of course, she isn't having sex in the picture. As the photo fades to black I can see the lace of another high collar. And the barest hint of her hands in motion. She's playing the piano. This has been sex for her. This is how a healthy young woman has managed to remain a virgin; not because she is sexless, but because she found a different sensual outlet for her body.

It's hard to tear my gaze away from that shot in the header. Distantly I recognize that it must have been taken by a professional photographer, the focus is too clear, the lighting too perfect, for anything less. There's a surprising streak of jealousy—that another man has been here, photographing her, admiring her, but I push that aside. All of this looks completely professional. The name across the top isn't hers, not precisely. A stage name. *Bea Sharp,* like the musical note. I have to blink once, twice, against the number of followers she has. This is more than an Internet sensation. This is a real-life celebrity sitting beside me, blushing profusely.

"It's a little strange seeing someone look at it," the celebrity says, her skin a pretty pink. "Normally I can just pretend like no one really sees me."

Many thousands of people see her, the numbers prove. Millions actually. "This is incredible. You do this from here. Where is the piano?"

She gestures toward the other side of the suite. "The second bedroom. It was always the music room, but since the page has grown, I have some lighting equipment and cameras."

My finger hovers over one of the videos. "May I?"

"You don't have to," she says, which doesn't answer the question.

"It's rather embarrassing how much I want to. But only with your permission."

She ducks her head in a picture of humble grace. My God, this woman. She is from a different time period, one with gowns and thrones. No wonder she lives at the top of the tower. So what would that make me? A court jester, I suppose. Someone to amuse her.

The video expands on the screen, focused on the piano. Only a little of her body is visible, a deep velvet dress that ends halfway down her forearms. Her nails are unpolished, neatly trimmed, square-tipped but delicate, strong and feminine. Her skin gleams in the bright light, highlighting the freckles across her skin, even there. I like to think that if I had seen this video first, I would have recognized her by her hands alone, both delicate and surprisingly strong.

On the screen she places her hands on the piano.

In real life she twines her fingers together, anxious and anticipatory.

Both of the actions make a knot in my chest, tight enough that it's hard to breathe. I can't take a breath until the first note reverberates through the air. Even through the pale phone speakers I can feel the depth of the sound. The undeniable rightness of it.

And then she plays, bringing to life Sia's "Chandelier" with a classical bent that I can only marvel at. I can feel her skill and her passion coming through every note. There is reckless abandon in the song, fear and grief and hope. "*Mon Dieu*," I breathe.

From the corner of my eye, in the single ounce of my body not focused wholly on the song being played, I can see Bea's fingers twitch in the same pattern they do on screen. She really is in her element with music. She's a goddess.

I set the phone down, letting it play between us.

The notes build something new between us, a kind of foreplay. When she looks at me, I can tell she feels it too. This time she isn't afraid. It isn't something to fear, the music.

"Bea," I murmur. "Come here."

She does not hesitate. In seconds she's in my arms, and I pull her firmly onto my lap. There's only a slight squirm, enough to make my cock throb, while she wonders whether I can support her. Why do women worry about that? There's nothing more fulfilling than holding her this way, than feeling her soft and supple in my arms while I hold her still for a kiss.

My lips touch hers with barely held restraint. *Don't devour her.*

The music is her tutor this time, but it's also mine. It teaches us the rhythm to use as I nip gently at her bottom lip, as she shyly strokes her tongue against mine.

When she pulls back, she's breathing hard. Those pale green eyes are darker now, with passion, with confidence, and I am close to bursting.

"Wow," she whispers.

It makes me laugh a little, though it comes out unsteady. *Mon Dieu,* indeed.

You might think that I must woo every client, but most frequently it happens the other way around. Women tempt me and flatter me and please me, even when they are paying for the privilege. I have been treated to the finest chefs and flown in private jets. They wear beautiful lingerie and compliment me as if I might walk out the door if they don't.

Nothing has ever seduced me as much as this.

No one as much as her.

"Can we do it again?" she asks, a little playful.

Why did I think I could be the court jester for her? I would be the peasant, not even fit to set a foot in the same room. "I want to lick you," I tell her, fervent and true. "Kneeling before you while you play this song for me."

Her eyes widen, because she does not mistake my meaning. "I'm sure I couldn't keep playing."

"You'll have lots of practice first," I say, and I don't mean practice playing the piano.

I mean practice receiving pleasure from my tongue, her legs spread wide for me, her pussy wet and swollen from my caresses. I want her so well versed in this that she begs me with her subtle little moans, barely audible above the song. It's a physical pain, imagining her hips jerk against me as she climaxes, the singular vibration of the keys as she comes.

Her eyes have turned a beautiful shade of green, darker than jade. It makes me think of a smooth lake lit by a full moon, both opaque and luminescent.

"Again," I murmur.

Can we do it again? It's startling how much I want that. Not only to kiss her but to hold her, to *see* her. There's a longing inside me to ask to see her again, even though it shouldn't matter if she books another Saturday night, shouldn't matter if it's her or any other woman. It's never mattered before.

This time she is the one to press her lips to mine, and it's that much sweeter. With her uncertainty and her eagerness. I have never experienced anything this wholesome. I certainly did not expect to find it in a client.

She does not move to open her mouth, nor open mine. There's only the press, somehow made more erotic by the chasteness. I surrender to it, surrender to *her*, glorying in the sensation of plump lips and feather breaths. The sensation of her trembling body in my arms, the shimmer of moonlight on water made real.

Her body shifts on my lap, barely an inch to the side. Enough to brush against my hard cock. I suck in a breath, shocked by the effort it takes not to come.

She barely touched me. She *didn't* touch me,

not on purpose. There are so many layers of clothes between us, but I'm ready to come like a teenager.

Her eyes meet mine, wide and wondering. "Is that…"

"My cock. Say it. I want to hear you say the word."

A blush. "Right now?"

"If you want it inside you, you should be able to ask for it."

"Cock," she whispers.

I'm moved by her shyness and by how much she wants me. Moved by the sweet curiosity in her trembling voice. But not enough to let her off the hook. "Say 'I want your cock.'"

There's a longer pause this time. "I want your cock."

Jesus, my cock throbs in response. It hears her. It wants her right back. "Say 'Make me come on your cock, until my pretty little cunt can't take any more.'"

She sucks in a breath. "This is what you meant."

"What?"

"About desire."

"Haven't you felt it before, *mon amie*? Why did you call for me if not for desire?"

It's a question she has dodged before, her reasons. And she dodges it again. "Not like this. I wondered. I was curious, but I never felt it like this."

I force myself to observe her coolly, from a distance instead of like the slavering beast I feel inside. "Breathing hard, eyelids low. You're warm all over. Yes, this is what desire looks like. And I'm sure you'll be wet when I touch you, won't you?"

She exhales, a sound of acquiescence. "Make me come on your cock."

"Until?" Perhaps it is cruel of me. The knowledge isn't enough to make me stop. That's how badly I want to hear those words from her petal-pink mouth.

"Until my pretty little pussy can't take any-more."

Hearing the words from her lips is too much. I have to kiss her, and once I start, I can't stop. I'm tasting her, licking her, biting her. Her enthusiasm matches my own; she tugs at my shirt, my collar, trying to get closer. It's not enough, never enough.

There's a moment of indecision, when her knee comes up, blocking us. It's now that I should take us to the bedroom. Now that I should turn this frantic make-out session into a seduction. But my own need burns too hotly. I'm wild and untried, as if her inexperience has become my own. So I yank her onto my lap, harder, fully against me. And then she straddles me, her heat pressed right up against my cock. There's no slowing this down. No stopping.

She moves her hips against me, hesitant, curious. "Is this okay?"

"It's perfect. Do it again."

When she does, I'm the one who lets out a groan. *Mon Dieu*, her body is heaven. I'm torn between the places I want to touch her—to cup her face and feel her hair curl around my hand. To feel her breasts, maybe find the buttons hidden in the demure lace dress and bare her to me.

I decide on her hips, the better to rock her pussy against my cock. I'm throbbing and hurting, but all I want is for her to come. I show her the rhythm, and there, *there*, she learns it.

Her frantic little breaths flutter against my neck like a butterfly. Every muscle in my body strains against the need to throw her onto the table, the dishes and seduction be damned. There is self-control somewhere inside me. I don't *feel* it, but it must be there, because somehow I remain seated, barely, my whole body clenching, hips already fucking into nothing.

When she comes, I feel her ecstasy wash over me like a balm. It doesn't feel *good*. That would be too ordinary for someone like Bea. It feels like I've been granted a reprieve.

I hold her against me as the tremors take her body, one hand keeping her hips flush with mine, the other cradling her head on my shoulder.

Distantly I realize I'm muttering to her in Arabic. Strange, that. It's the language I used on the streets of Tangier. The one of familiarity and abandon. I'm alternately soothing her and cursing her, though I'm sure she can understand neither.

Slowly she stills. Her breathing evens out.

When she lifts her head, there's a distinct echo of loss in my chest.

"Is this...okay?" Her pale green eyes are large now, still hazy from sex but with some worry seeping in. Perhaps she senses that I'm *not* okay.

Perhaps because I'm clenching her ass hard enough to leave fingerprint bruises.

It's an act of extreme hardship and heroism that I let go of her. I'm not entirely graceful as I shove her off my lap. Not entirely steady on my feet, but *mon Dieu*. My cock is as hard as iron in my pants, leaking against the black fabric, ready to explode.

If this were an ordinary relationship, I would take it out. Let her talented little fingers stroke me the way she plays the piano. Let her pretty lips taste me, but this isn't an ordinary relationship. I've had women blow me, of course. Many clients wish to. Some even want me like this, desperate and demanding. But they are experienced enough to ask for it. This woman, she's too innocent for the thoughts in my head. So I force myself to the bathroom.

I force out the words to say, *excuse me,* but I'm too far gone to be sure. They might be in English or French. Or in Arabic, the street language, the one I mumble in dreams.

Only in private do I lean my back against the door and pull down my zipper. There is infinite relief, letting my heavy cock fall onto my palm.

It only takes two strokes, remembering the spice on her tongue, the softness of her lips. The sweetness of her body in my arms. And I'm coming, spurting into my hand.

In the aftermath I can only stare at the gold-plated bathroom fixtures, the tile that is probably imported from Paris itself, with faded script and designs on every other piece.

I know I should not, but I have never been

very wise. And so my head turns to the side, where I can see myself in the mirror. My hair is askew. My cheeks dark with passion. I look like a man who has been months without sex, years without it.

Like a man who has only just discovered what it is.

CHAPTER TEN

W HEN I RETURN, the dining room is empty.
Except for the cat, who sits and watches me with judgment in her gray eyes. Does she smell Bea's desire in the air? Does she smell mine? Of course she does; she's a cat. Why do I care? I can't help but want her to like me, this scared little girl with razor-sharp claws.

I peek into the bedroom, but the white sheets are neat and tidy. I'm half-tempted to check behind the dresser, as if Bea might have shoved herself into a corner.

And then the music starts.

Like the kind that came streaming over the Internet, but far better than anything the tiny speakers in my phone could have reproduced. The sound draws me back through the living room to the other end of the penthouse.

I pause at the doorway, uncertain of my welcome.

Notes filter through the cracked doorway.

More than anyone, I know that true privacy comes not from the body but from the mind. She might not want me in the room.

In the end it's my own need that decides me. I need to see her, to feel her. To make sure she's okay. We didn't do anything particularly traumatic. A dry-humping session is practically adolescent, but I find myself strangely protective of her. Protective even from myself.

The door is silent as I push it open, revealing a room with a grand piano in the middle, lighting and video equipment all around the edges. There's a large black rectangle in the corner with a hundred silver switches on it, as if she's going to fly to the moon.

Bea sits at the piano, her eyes closed as her fingers dance over the keys.

The music stops.

Her eyes light up as she sees me, and I can finally take a deep breath.

"There you are," she says, a little playful.

I like her like this, relaxed. It's the music that makes her this way, but I like to think that it was me, too. Her orgasm, the one she wrung from my body.

"Here I am," I say, wandering into the room, careful not to step on any wires. "This is quite an elaborate setup. Do you know what all these machines do?"

A smile flickers at the edges of her lips. "It was either that or get a filming crew every day."

"You post every day?" I already know that I'll be checking her channel from home, a level of connection I've never had with any client before, never wanted.

"Most days."

"Do the other musicians mind? When you play their songs?"

"Some." A small shrug. "Now it's a big enough business that I can license the songs that I want to show. And before that…"

She plays a little song. It takes me a moment to realize it's the refrain from "Baby, One More Time" by Britney Spears. Considering why I'm here, I can't help the smile that spreads. She's a dangerous woman, this one. Already beautiful and smart and shy. And now, funny?

Dangerous.

"Before that?"

"Before that I was lucky. This really huge artist saw one of my videos and she reposted it. Then it happened again with someone else. Next thing I knew I had these big PR firms contacting me, wanting me to do one of their client's songs as soon as it comes out."

I lean one hip against the piano, looking down at her. I'm the one above her, but she's still the goddess on her glossy black bench. Lucky? That wasn't luck. That was her incredible talent and what must be serious business intelligence. "And if you don't like the song?"

"Then I don't play it. But that's not really the test. It's more about whether I think I can add something to the song, something to make it my own. I wouldn't just play the song as written. So if I don't feel it... on the inside, you know? If I don't have something to add, I won't take the deal."

"That's incredible," I tell her. "That you've built this empire in your spare bedroom. You can pick and choose what you play. Make it your own. I'm in awe of you."

A breathy little laugh that I feel all the way in my soul. "It feels like me alone in a room, most days. Which is the only reason I can do it."

So much isolation. Does it cost her something? I think it does, even if she doesn't know it. "Would you ever play in front of an audience?'

"Oh no," she says immediately. "I could never. Not only because I wouldn't leave, but... playing is private. The cameras aren't real people.

They're just recording. Not watching."

An interesting distinction, but I'm not convinced. There are thousands of people watching those videos. Bea may tell herself she's alone, that she prefers it that way, but it hurts her. And for some reason I think I can help with this problem. A foolish idea, probably.

You're falling for her, asshole.

"Has it always been like this for you? Creating new songs from what you hear?"

She shakes her head. "I mean, I always heard the music in my head. I thought that was normal. My mom was the same way. She was a concert pianist." I hear the pride in her voice. "She played in Carnegie Hall."

"That's incredible."

A shaky breath moves her. "She died, when I was nine. My dad, too."

Everything inside me goes still. This is huge. An earthquake in the middle of afternoon tea. What she's revealing to me splits her world apart. It's splitting mine.

"It was…pirates, actually." This time her laugh is pained. Bitter. The kind that slices through my defenses. How many people has she told this to? Not many. Maybe no one. "They were on a yacht. A party with a hundred people, but the pirates only took them."

"Why?" I breathe, but I already know the answer. It's folded around us. Money.

"They wanted a ransom. At least that's what they usually did, but something must have gone wrong. They usually would have only taken my mom, made my dad pay the ransom. But for whatever reason that day they took them both."

And they didn't come back. "Bea. You don't have to continue."

Her eyes are mournful. "But I do, because you do something to me. Make me feel open and vulnerable. Scared, but like I want to keep feeling it. How do you do that?"

You do that to me, too. I don't say it.

"They never found out exactly what happened on that boat. Probably my dad fought them. There was a struggle and both of them died that day, before they even asked for anything."

"I'm sorry, Bea." More sorry than I can put into words. More sorry than I thought I could feel for someone. On the streets of Tangier I saw more tragedy than should exist, but it moves me beyond bearing, her suffering.

She gives a little shake of her head. "Most of the time I don't think of it."

"Why now?" I ask softly.

She scrunches her nose. "This is embarrassing but I guess it's talking to you. I mean, using words. I go downstairs and chat with people, but it's always on the surface. Anything deep, anything important, it happens through music."

"It's beautiful," I tell her when what I mean is, *you're beautiful.*

"When they died, I stopped speaking."

"You mean… entirely?"

"For a couple years, yeah. There were therapists and doctors. I could make a sound, if I was startled or scared. But I didn't form words. I already played piano before that, but after that it was the only way I would communicate. Anything I wanted to express, it happened here."

I understand that she means more than the piano. She means this room.

God.

Chords of longing and loneliness fill the air, her expression dark.

"'Hotel California,'" I say softly.

Then her eyes brighten. "For you."

This one I recognize immediately. 'Castle on a Cloud.' It's a song that's part of the Les Misérables musical. My face turns to stone, but inside there's a clamor.

The notes slow and then stop.

"Sorry. Was that weird? Because your name is Hugo. And the author was Victor Hugo." She looks crestfallen. "Of course that was dumb."

I force myself to speak through the chaos inside me. "Not dumb."

"Then why do you look like you're going to throw up."

Moving stiffly, I manage to sit next to her on the bench. She scoots to the side to make room for me. "I'm sorry," I say.

"No, don't. I'm the one who can't interact with regular people."

"I hope you aren't categorizing me as *regular*," I tell her, managing to find some wry humor in this situation. I want to shut down, to push her away, but she opened herself up too far for that. "The truth is that my mother named me for that author."

Green eyes widen. "Did she?"

"I'm not sure why I'm named Hugo instead of Victor. Perhaps because it was easier to spell." Then I admit something that always pained Mama. "She couldn't read."

She couldn't read, so she never knew the irony of a book about a man starved enough to steal bread and a revolution he wouldn't need. About a whore who sacrificed for her daughter and a grand love she would never know.

"But she liked the story?" Bea asks, too inno-cent to realize that there was no one else on our street who could read either. No one knew the story, but Mama kept the large book as a sad little tribute to our French heritage. Only when I moved to America did I learn what it was about.

"She liked that it was long and important." Perhaps she thought it would help me become important, instead of an illiterate maid. I never knew what my father did for a living. My skin is darker than Mama's, my hair a rich black. So my father was probably native to Morocco, one of the transient workers who appeared and disappeared like ghosts haunting the harbor.

"I'm named after an author too," Bea says. "But her books were less long. Less important, too."

"Who?"

"Beatrix Potter." At my look of bemusement she explains. "She wrote *Peter Rabbit*. It's a children's book about a rabbit who gets into trouble."

"It sounds less tragic, at least."

She laughs a little, but sadly. "That's true. Will you come back next week, Hugo?"

I have the feeling this question is about more

than money, but that's the only way I know how to answer. "Of course, darling. Call the agency and get on my schedule."

CHAPTER ELEVEN

AT THE BEGINNING I worked most nights. I shared a one-room apartment with Sutton, who arrived in Tanglewood more broke than myself. Every cent I earned went into investments, some throughout the city in real estate, others in the stock market. As my portfolio grew and my hourly rate got higher, I stopped working—except for Saturday nights.

Even with a large nest egg, the money I make in a single evening is worthwhile. My services are only for the elite women of the city, those who can afford to throw thousands of dollars at pleasure.

And I enjoy my time, usually.

The arrangement suits me, but not everyone is pleased. When a knock comes on my door Sunday morning, I know who it is before I check the security camera on my phone.

It is with great reluctance that I press the button to let her in.

I take a final swallow of espresso before I get up to meet her at the door. We exchange kisses on the cheek, superficial pleasantries before she attempts to stab me in the back.

"Come in," I tell her genially, because I have much experience with pretending.

Melissande gives me a dark look because she knows this. "Beatrix Cartwright booked you again."

I stroll into the living room and recline on one of the over-plush leather sofas. Everything here is luxurious and modern and completely impersonal. The furnished loft was only going to be a stepping stone after moving out of Sutton's, but I've never seen any reason to leave.

"I thought you'd be pleased." This is a lie. Nothing has pleased her for many years.

She sits across from me, crossing her slender legs, revealing the edges of her garters. Always dressed to impress, this woman. "Meanwhile the rest of your clients are clamoring for an appointment. This new girl is taking up all your time."

"So give the night to someone else," I say, pretending my throat isn't tight at the thought of not seeing Bea again. But I've never minded who booked my time before. I'm not going to start now, especially when Melissande would see it for the weakness it is.

"Beatrix pays too well," she says, looking annoyed despite the fact that she makes a neat forty percent for doing nothing but taking phone calls.

"Then why are you here?"

"You know why. Because you need to work more nights."

"*Non,* I'm doing very well. You are the one who needs me to work more nights."

A sneer forms on her pretty lips. "Are you having trouble keeping it up more than once a week? There are medicines that can help with that."

It does not bother me, the insult. She used to be a whore before she became the madam. And like most women her hourly rates only went down and down. While mine only goes up. It is the curse of our genders, but I will not quibble over it. "I work Saturday nights. That's all."

At my quiet certainty, her face forms a pout. I'm sure that is effective on some men. Once it would have been effective on me, but I learned not to trust her a long time ago.

Her dark gaze takes me in, from my open collar to my fresh slacks to my bare feet. I am only beginning the day, still comfortable and crisp.

Her eyes heat in that familiar way that once would have made the back of my neck warm. Now I'm left completely cold.

"Or perhaps I can remind you of what it felt like to have sex every night. Several times a night. You were quite skilled at that, once. Maybe that was only for me."

"I was fifteen," I say, my voice flat. "And horny."

Rage flashes in her eyes. "Don't be crass, darling."

I manage not to flinch when she says that. *Darling.* That's where I learned it, after all. A word to push someone away. "You know very well that I can leave you whenever I please and earn the same amount of money. More, probably."

She smiles, probably not realizing how cruel it looks. "Then why don't you?"

Melissande was a beautiful woman when I met her, in the finest designer clothes and with her glossy hair in curls. She had so much money, I could not have guessed that she was a prostitute for the wealthy men who came to the city. She took me into her penthouse suite and showed me what it meant to be a man—or at least what I thought it meant.

There was nothing keeping me in Tangier, so

when she offered me the chance to come with her to America, I took it. Perhaps it should have alarmed me that we had to pretend I was her adopted son in the paperwork, but I was too eager to come. Too blindly in love.

My lips twist in a wry smile. "Perhaps because I still have feelings for you."

Her cheeks flush, most likely with anger. She hates to be the subject of pity. But what else can I feel for her? When I realized she only wanted to whore me out, it broke my heart. There are no feelings left in that organ now. No love and no warmth.

"I'll give you seventy percent," she says flatly.

"Thank you," I say. "I will be happy to accept seventy percent of what Beatrix pays for Saturday night. But no more than that. One night a week. That's all you get."

She narrows her eyes. "There's something different about this girl, isn't there?"

"Apparently she pays more," I say, my voice dry.

"No, something else. Is her pussy extra tight? She did mention her little problem. The virginity thing. I told her you would take care of that. Did it feel special, Hugo?"

It's been years since her digs could make me

angry. And yet I feel it rising inside me now, the need to tell her not to talk about Bea. It would only give Melissande power.

"But no, I have not even fucked her yet."

Her eyes widen, her surprise real instead of manufactured. "Why not?"

"Perhaps because I'm making *her* fall in love with *me*. After all, I did learn from the best."

CHAPTER TWELVE

"**D**IM SUM," I tell her, twirling the last sip of wine in the glass. We're having dinner again downstairs in Beau Ciel, because it's the only restaurant she can visit. *For now.* "They have dumplings with pork and lotus root. It comes fresh from the kitchen, still steaming as they bring it around to the tables."

It feels explicit to describe this food to her, especially the way her eyes have turned soft and sensual, the sage green she gives me when she's going to come. "Don't," she whispers.

"You pick one up with your chopsticks. Have you used chopsticks before? No matter, you can use your fingers. The dumpling will be soft and round, but tightly held. You can bring it to your lips and—"

She makes a squeak. There's no other word for the sound. Like a mouse. "I can't go. I want to, I mean I *really* want to, but it's not as simple as that."

"But no, I can have my car pulled around in two minutes flat."

"I would have a panic attack."

I can tell from the earnestness in her voice that she believes this. However I can also tell that she needs to overcome this, that she will never fully be living until she does. It's not only the fact of her existence in L'Etoile's marble walls. Perhaps another woman would be content here. It's the hunger in her eyes that becomes stronger every time I speak of a new thing she could experience if she left.

Bea must leave, and somehow I've made it my mission to have her do it.

"Is there something we could do for a panic? Perhaps a breathing technique. Or a medicine."

She's already shaking her head. "There's nothing."

I give her a dubious look. "How can you be sure? They have many advancements. And when is the last time you tried to leave?"

She picks at her steak. From here I can see that it's perfectly cooked. Juicy. And completely terrible to a woman who can have only this and a small menu besides. "It may have been a while, but that's only because I learned my boundaries. I remember how it felt."

"And how was that?"

"Like dying."

That is no small feat to overcome, then. "Have I told you about the little shop off Fifth Street? They serve a green tea gelato pressed between two fresh lavender macarons."

Her eyes are darker again. It's the sex look. I've been dreaming about it. My nights are filled with moss and fog. I'm searching for something, for someone, but never satisfied.

"I'll have it delivered," she says.

I give her a look. "Non. You will have melting gelato and soggy cookies."

"You don't understand."

"So explain it to me. You must have some kind of doctor, yes? What does he say?"

"I have a psychologist, yes. She comes to visit me once a month."

"This time you will explain you wish to leave."

Her eyes narrow. "You're very bossy."

I take her hand from across the table. "I would not dare to boss you. I only want to help. The way you look at me, it seems like you want that, too."

She sighs. "Oh yes. Yes. But it's impossible."

Building an incredible celebrity without ever

leaving this building, that's impossible. Hiring an overpriced escort to take her sweet virginity, impossible. This woman does impossible things.

A sudden stroke of inspiration has me sitting up straight. "What about a piano? Don't you wish to play on pianos other than your own?"

Her stricken expression is almost enough to stop me. Almost.

"Bellmont," comes a low voice behind me.

I turn, startled to recall that we aren't alone. There's Damon Scott, the proprietor of the Den. He's a powerful and dangerous man in this city. And apparently one of the diners at Beau Ciel tonight.

My stomach tightens. I have been seen with my clients before. Of course I have. In some ways I am like an expensive crocodile leather purse. I am the toy breed dog they carry inside. Something to show how wealthy and fabulous they are. There is no shame for them, or for me, but Bea is different.

If they give her a snide look, I'm not sure what I will do. Nothing good.

But the woman on Damon Scott's arm—I remember her name, Penny—she smiles at us. "Did I hear you mention pianos? We have a beautiful Blüthner grand in the library. I can't play, but we keep it tuned in case someone else can."

Bea's lips form an O of undisguised longing. "That would be incredible, but… I really can't. I'm sorry."

Damon smiles genially, though he must remember my profession. And he must guess who Bea is to me. "It's perfectly fine. Anytime you wish to come, have Hugo bring you."

"Thank you," I tell him softly.

"A friend of yours is a friend of ours," Damon answers at the same volume.

I could not say what Bea is to me. A friend? A lover? But she is more than just a client, and I have not even taken her virginity yet. What will happen when I breach her hymen? It should be a purely physical act, but I'm discovering more and more that nothing is ever as simple as it seems with her.

"Bea is a very talented musician," I tell them.

"Oh, it must run in the family," Penny says brightly. All three of us stare at her for a surprised beat, and her lips twist. "Did I say something wrong?"

"How did you know?" I manage to ask, because Bea looks too shocked to respond.

Penny scrunches her nose. "Was I not supposed to say anything? I'm sorry. It's just that your father was so amazing. His work on computational lexicon is basically legend. I read his biography so I know about his wife and that he had a daughter. I shouldn't have said anything."

"No, it's fine," Bea assures her, recovering her voice. "Truly. I was only surprised because people don't usually recognize me unless they see my full name."

"You have his eyes," Penny says as if offering a confession.

That makes Bea smile a little. "I know. And thank you for remembering him this way. It's really such a gift that you remember him for the good in his life instead of..."

Instead of his tragic death.

Damon clears his throat. "I'll see you at the Den, Bellmont?"

"Tomorrow," I murmur, unable to take my eyes from Bea's melancholy expression.

And then we are alone. "Who's your father?" I ask softly.

"Arthur Cartwright."

I know him immediately, though I never would have linked the tech magnate with Silicon Valley origins to the timid young woman trapped in a tower in Tanglewood. "The inventor."

She nods. "The only thing he loved more than his work was my mother."

"I'm sorry," I say, knowing the memories are dark.

"I meant what I said. I'm glad that he can be remembered for the things he accomplished. I don't think I've lived up to the family name, anyway. Not with the way I'm stuck here. The way I panic at even the thought of going outside."

"We can go to the Den. I would stay with you every second."

She laughs, though the sound wrenches my heart. "It's impossible, Hugo."

I do not argue with words, but she knows my thoughts.

"Come upstairs," she offers, and my arguments evaporate into nothing. There is only her offer and the powerful knowledge in her eyes. *Tonight.*

CHAPTER THIRTEEN

THE FIRST TIME I was in this bedroom I rescued her kitty. The second time I made her come. Both of those times I wanted to help Bea, but this time is completely different. It's my own need that drives me as I lead her by the hand to the bed. The need to undress her and feel her naked skin against my own. It's a wild animal inside me, this need. Gnashing and growling with hunger.

She's trembling. I feel the tremors where my hand holds hers. There's uncertainty in her eyes, enough to give me pause. Not enough to make me stop. I undress her with slow deliberation, undoing the small buttons at her back, then the zipper the rest of the way, revealing so much covered skin that I feel drunk with it.

Make this good for her.

I never have to remind myself of that. It's always my primary purpose. From the very beginning, sex has been a way to make a woman feel beautiful, feel pleasure. Only now does it seem like something else.

She wears a white lace bra, which I remove from her body an inch at a time, placing an almost chaste kiss to every inch revealed. Her white lace panties go next, but I don't kiss her there. Not yet. Not when she's looking at me like I'm going to ravish her, a little worried.

Desire beats a heavy drum in my veins. This time it's different because I want to touch her more than I want her to be touched. I want to fuck her more than she wants to be fucked. I want *her…*

More than she wants me.

I'm wild with this wanting, my hands too rough, my breathing harsh.

There's something primal about what's happening to me. It's out of my control, the way I push her back onto the bed, the way I slide between her legs, the way I push my cock against her. There are still clothes between us, but I have no intention of letting her grind against me to completion like we did in the dining room. The only way this ends is with me pulsing inside her wet heat.

"I'm nervous," she whispers, her eyes an opaque jade green.

"I won't hurt you."

There may not be any of my usual finesse, but I'll make her come hard enough to see stars. The way the ceiling of Beau Ciel lights up, pinpricks of white on a painted blue swirl.

She gives me a quick grin, full of mischief. "What if I hurt you?"

Mon Dieu, I'm already aching. How much more can I take? "You don't need to worry about me. You never need to worry. There's only your beautiful body."

And I need to feel her against me, naked and warm, so I pull back enough to unbutton my white dress shirt and push down my slacks. My boxer briefs are left, and I consider leaving them on for her comfort. But I'd rather she know what she's getting into.

So I strip completely, releasing my cock, heavy and dark with arousal.

Her gaze darts away, skittish now. And when she looks back at me, I have the sensation I had when her kitty looked up at me from behind the dresser. "I know I'm not who you would be with, not really, but I still want to make this good for you. If there's something I should do, you have to tell me."

My heart pounds. Not who I would be with?

Her hair curls wildly around her head, framing her pale face, decorating the pillow. Her lashes are the same copper color, fanning around those pretty eyes. Her eyebrows are a shade darker, two crescents I want to trace with my thumb. And then there's her nose. Should there be any allure to a nose? It's a utilitarian feature, not a form of seduction. But hers is small and curving up, a reminder of the innocence that brought me to her. Her lips are full and plush. I want to sink into them.

Not who I would be with?

If I wanted to be with her any more than this, I would expire on the spot.

"For that," I say, pressing a kiss to a cluster of freckles at the corner of her eye, "I will have to make you come so hard you cannot think. There's no other solution to such a claim."

Her eyes widen. "What? No, you don't have to—"

"And when I'm licking you and drinking you down, lapping every drop with a hunger so great, you won't be able to doubt how much I want you, how beautiful I find you."

Her breath catches, which is better than self-doubt. I don't want doubt anywhere near her. Only the confidence she has when she plays at the piano, all the time.

I move down her body one constellation at a time, stroking her skin, pressing a quick kiss. Laving her with my tongue. Her freckles are pale on pale, almost an optical illusion. I can only see them under certain light, so I move her body as I go, lifting her hips, touching her so that she arches up toward my mouth. When I'm at the top of her sex, she presses her legs together.

I'm so starved for her. Can't she see that? But no, she's busy thinking of how she looks. Wondering if I like the bronze hair or the porcelain skin. It seems impossible that she doesn't know.

It almost seems impossible that she's real.

"Let me taste you, sweet Bea. I won't force you, but I want you bad enough that it hurts me inside. I'm imagining how you taste, how you'll feel on my tongue. The way you'll clench when you come. And it's a physical pain." I put a hand to my breastbone so she'll know where. There are barbs. "You are the most beautiful woman I've ever seen. Let me in."

Her eyes close briefly as if in prayer. "How do you do this?"

"What?"

"How do you make me believe it?"

I want to say more, but then she opens her legs for me, and the sight is enough to render me speechless. The pain becomes a driving spear inside me until I bend down and lick her deep at her core. She gasps, a sound of shock and pleasure, so I do it again.

"You taste like sweetness and sex, Bea." I don't have the willpower to lift my mouth from her completely, so my words come out muffled, but I think she understands. Her hips press up, asking for more, and I run my tongue along the ridge of her sex. "My cock is as hard as it's ever been. I'm pressing it into the sheets for relief, but it doesn't help."

A soft moan. "Hugo."

I kiss an openmouthed trail up to her clit. "And right here, this sweet bud. I've been dreaming about it and look at you. Even your sex is shy, hiding from me. Uncertain."

It needs to be reassured, like the woman beneath me, so I press my tongue flat against her bud. Her whole body goes tense and quivering, and I have to hold her down at her hips. She only has enough room to nudge her body up, up, up. I wait for her to realize this, to try it out, to feel the mind-melting pleasure of it. I'm not licking her at this moment; I'm letting her fuck my tongue.

"You're so beautiful," she murmurs.

I realize I've closed my eyes, the taste of her so incredible I want to memorize it. Because this won't last forever. How can it? She will move on to a man equal of her, and I will be left with a hollow loft and a cold madam. There's only now.

The corner of my lip kicks up. "Beautiful?"

She laughs a little. "Are you offended? But you are. You're handsome, too. And strong. I mean, you have an actual six-pack. I thought those weren't even real."

The six-pack in question flexes against the mattress as if showing off for her. Working out is something of a requirement for this profession. It's also a pleasant way to pass the time, but now it seems imperative, as if I've been lifting and running and swimming all these years for this.

"But you're beautiful, too," she says, soft and hurting.

I press one final kiss to her clit and am rewarded with a whimper. Then I climb up her body, my cock leaking a line of precum along the sheets. "I wish to be beautiful for you, if that's what you want. And handsome. And strong."

When I'm close enough, she traces two fingers over my lips, which are still damp from her arousal. Her brow is furrowed in concentration, like maybe she's trying to memorize me too.

"Will you have sex with me now?" she asks, and I can't tell from her tone what answer she wants.

Somehow I find the condom in my wallet and tear the foil open, slipping the latex over my cock. "I think I'll die if I don't."

That makes her smile. "You're the only man I've ever wanted like this."

Those are the last words I hear before I notch my cock against her pussy and slide home. The pride wars with pleasure, a galaxy implosion in my chest. Her private walls stretch to accommodate me, but not far enough. It feels like a vise around my cock, and I shudder against the sensations.

Bea gasps and strains at the intrusion, her hands pushing weakly against my shoulders. Her hair in disarray, her face flushed. She's like wildflowers in full bloom across the valley. It makes me feel like the sun, beaming down on her, making her turn toward me.

"Too much," I say between gritted teeth.

It's not a question because I know I gave her too much and too fast. Her body trembles underneath me, struggling, maybe even in pain. I can't hurt her. *Mon Dieu*, I need to pull out.

Except that would be torture.

I drop my forehead to the pillow beside her, my body outside my control, my cock still hard and throbbing inside her. It's all I can do not to thrust again and again. "Forgive me."

She makes little panting noises. "I didn't know—"

"Didn't know what?" I ask, my jaw clenched hard, eyes shut tight. It's a terrible knot, our bodies together. Too tight for me to pull away. Pulled hard enough to hurt her.

"That it could actually be too big." A strange riff that might be laughter. Or maybe tears. "I thought it would always work. I mean, it *looked* big, but what do I know?"

"It will work," I assure her, pressing a kiss to her temple even while my lower body pushes hard to stay inside her. "Once you have more experience. I'm so sorry for hurting you. I am an animal. A savage. A brute."

"I did ask for it," she offers weakly.

"Not like this." She wanted my patience and skill. She *paid* for it, but she's getting a side of me I didn't even know existed. I press my open mouth against her collarbone, tasting the salty sweetness of her skin.

A small sound, almost pain, but her lips are parted. There's pleasure in her eyes, and I think that maybe she likes me this way. Not the way I'm a steel rod inside her, but the way I'm consuming her. And so I rock my hips gently against her, pressing my body against her clit.

Her hands unclench and fall back to the mattress. "So good."

It's like the scent of blood, the small proof of her pleasure. I'm a predator crouched over her, untamed, made ferocious by the taste of her. That's the only excuse for what happens next, when I hold her hips in place and find the angle that I know will release her entirely. And I pound into her swollen body with every ounce of my passion, no regard for her newly lost innocence.

In the reckless thrusts that follow I hit the place inside her body that makes her head fall back, her breasts push up, her legs open wider. "Oh my God."

Despite the intensity inside me, an unsteady laugh escapes me. "You are breathtaking. You are perfection. And I don't think I can ever leave your body."

For a moment she looks lost. "Is it always like this?"

In this moment there is only raw honesty. "It's never like this."

The thought terrifies me. This is supposed to

be new for her, not for me. Never for me.

Then her lips are under mine, her body pliant and accepting, and I am lost. There's only the drive to make her come, fucking into her until she moans and stiffens. "Yes," I mutter. "Again."

There's a faint protest, I think. *You don't have to*, she says, but she does not understand how much I want this. So I show her, with the unrelenting drive into her body, against the place inside her that makes her legs shake. She comes again and again, drenching my cock with her pleasure, testing unused muscles that might make her sore tomorrow.

I can't think about tomorrow, when I definitely won't be inside her. Won't be in this large bed. Won't be breathing in the air around Bea.

So I fuck her until her eyes are hazy with orgasms.

The jade green clears slightly, and she places a hand on my cheek, impossibly soft and not quite steady. "Aren't you going to?"

I don't know why I haven't already. I would have with any other woman, with any other *client*, after bringing her to climax a few times, if only to punctuate our evening. But I don't want this to end. As soon as I spill inside her, I have to leave.

Ripping my body away from her is an acute

pain, the cold air like razor blades on my cock. I grab one of the white pillows, feeling the abrasion of lace. There are two of them, enough to pad my beautiful girl as I turn her over.

"Oh," she says in lovely surprise.

There are a sprinkling of freckles coming down from her shoulders, like a shooting star fading into empty space. She's pale white down to her lovely ass, where she's peachy and flushed from my grasp. It's a beautiful sight, but I didn't flip her over to see this; I did it to hide myself.

"This will be an education," I murmur against her ear, my body covering her back. "That's why you wanted me, yes? Because of things I know. Things I can teach you."

Her moan is tortured pleasure. "Yes. Please. More."

I slide back into her as if her body was made for mine. She squeezes me in welcome, and it's enough to make me curse in Arabic under my breath. "My name," I tell her.

And thank the sweet Lord, she understands. "Hugo."

"Again," I say, reaching around to stroke two blunt fingers over her clit. She's slick and wet and warm, and I never want to leave this, never want to leave *her.*

"Hugo!" So low and breathy I feel the vibration in my cock.

"One more time, sweet Bea. For me. I want to feel you come like this."

Each one of my thrusts pushes out a little whimper from her; every strum of her clit makes her breath suck in. *Mon Dieu*, how am I going to last? Because I want one more.

I run the edge of my teeth along the curl of her ear and feel her shiver in response. "Do you know what it does to me? Having you like this? Helpless underneath me? I want to tear your pretty lace sheets into strips and tie you to the bedpost. I want to fuck you all night long, until we've made you come a hundred times. And even then it wouldn't be enough."

The words bring her close, but it's the bite of my teeth on her shoulder that sends her over the edge. She comes with a scream that makes me insane.

I want to come on her pale back, on her plush ass, on the pretty lace sheets. But I can't do that. This isn't about what I want. *This has never been about what I want.*

The pulse of her *chatte* is ecstasy on my cock, fierce even through the latex, and I come with sharp, bright-light bursts that seem to go on forever, longer than can be borne, until I collapse, wrung out on her sated body.

CHAPTER FOURTEEN

I'M ALONE AT the Den the next day, because we aren't going to meet again until Sunday. I could have called the other men in the Thieves Club, but that would have meant admitting how much last night meant to me. How hard it was to leave her with a kind but reserved, *That was lovely, darling.* So when someone sits down at the armchair beside me, I'm startled.

Damon Scott looks out the window at the blur of cars and glint of sunlight. He does not ask permission before taking the seat, because he owns the place. Though I'm not sure he asks permission for anything, regardless. Except perhaps to his pretty lady friend.

We sit in silence in the way that only men can do. A woman would have asked me twenty questions by now. And normally I could field them with charm and seduction. Right now I'm only fit to brood.

"Beatrix Cartwright," he says. "You didn't

know?"

"That she was rich, yes. Not about her family."

"More than rich. She has one of the largest portfolios in the country. I knew she lived in Tanglewood, but I never met her before last night."

"She doesn't get out much," I say, my voice bland because I don't wish to share the details of her personal struggle with this man, even if the information might be worth something to him.

"Because of her guardian? That's what I always assumed."

My curiosity is piqued despite myself. Her guardian. The missing link between when she lived in a mansion in California and when she was planted in a penthouse in Tanglewood. The person who must have raised her after her parents were killed.

Someone who must know the owner of L'Etoile.

"Who is she?" I ask, but it's impossible not to appear interested. Not when I've been searching for this for so long. I'm leaning forward in my chair, any pretense of being casual long gone. There is a burn in my body, like acid. It fills every inch of my skin, singeing me from the inside out.

The fire is revenge.

Damon doesn't look surprised, as if he knew I would want to know. Perhaps he did. He's that kind of man. Dangerous to someone who would cross him. "Her parents were both isolated. Both only children. There was no extended family to take her in."

"Her name." I'm gritting my teeth against demanding more, now, faster.

"It's a man, actually. I've met him a few times."

A man. Why does that make me uncomfortable?

Perhaps because he has her locked up in a damned tower, so afraid of men she had to pay one to take her virginity. Or perhaps because he let her hide herself from the time she was a child instead of helping her recover from her parents' death.

"Is he a member here?"

"Yes, although he does not come frequently. I could introduce you."

That would be... exceptional, considering I would no longer need to use Bea for that purpose. Would she find out? That depends on how much this guardian, this man, has done. "What would it cost me?"

Damon only smiles. He does not refute the claim that he will charge me something, because we both know that this is a place of business. "I'm not certain it's a price you're willing to pay."

"Ah, money. How crude."

"It *is* how I'm accustomed to doing business. I'm sure you know that."

"It's not the cost I was referring to, however. What if you had to choose between Beatrix and finding this person? What if you had to choose between Beatrix and revenge?"

I sit up straight. It's one thing for him to guess at my curiosity; another thing for him to know the source. Hearing her name makes a strange possessiveness rise in me. Possessiveness and pain, at the idea of losing her. "How the fuck do you know what I want with the owner of L'Etoile?"

"Do you know what I sell, Hugo?"

"People," I say, because Damon is known to own strip clubs in the city. Many of them. High-end ones. And he held a virginity auction in the Den once.

"And how would I sell people without infor-mation? That's the leverage I truly need to run my business. Which is how I know about the discreet inquiries you've made."

"Not discreet enough."

"I'm rather a special case, if you don't mind me saying so. Most people won't know."

"Well, I hope you don't plan on selling me to the highest bidder. I'm afraid my virginity is long lost."

"Lost early, if I had to guess."

"I'd rather you didn't. Guess, that is." I was fifteen when I lost my virginity, though it didn't feel like a loss at the time. It felt like I had won something—a beautiful, glamorous woman. "If you have information to sell me, then sell it. But don't think that you will leverage me, because I have enough people doing that."

"The beautiful Melissande."

Of course he would know her.

Perhaps I had been too young. At fifteen I had felt like a man. Had been built like one after working summers in the field. Mama had been gone two years before then. Breast cancer, caught far too late, and with far too little money to do anything about it. There had only been enough to buy Valium to ease her pain toward the end.

I had been young, but I'd grown up early.

"Beautiful indeed," I say grimly.

"I want her out of business," Damon says, his voice flat and final.

That's his price, I realize. It really won't be a sum of money I can pull from my investment accounts. It will be a person that I must sell in order to achieve my revenge. "Why?"

"Does it matter?"

"Perhaps."

"Would it make you feel better if I said there was a noble reason? That she is a danger to Tanglewood and the people inside it? That I care about this city more than money?"

"You are not a noble man."

He smiles. "No matter what Penny thinks, you are right. And so the real reason is much more simple than that. She's competition. And here is a way to get rid of her."

"I see." Melissande has done me no favors in this life, despite what she may think. I was too young to have sex with a woman in her late twenties, someone sophisticated and with an ulterior motive in bringing me to the states. She encouraged me to fall in love with her knowing I would be nothing but a pretty little commodity for her business.

But I also do not wish to harm her. There's a connection between us. She's the woman who took my virginity. And gave me a future in the process.

Damon's mouth twists in bitter understanding. "It's not so easy, is it?"

Hurting a person to further my own gains? Not easy.

Then again it was not easy for my mother to clean soiled sheets and toilets for rich gamblers in Tangier. It was not easy for her to trudge two blocks before dawn only to return after nightfall, her muscles trembling with exhaustion.

It was not easy when one of those gamblers followed her home.

"A name would not be enough," I say.

Damon nods as if he expected that. "The means to ruin him."

I would only wish to ruin him if he's the man who pushed in the door when I was seven years old. The man who shoved me into the closet while my mother shrieked, blocked me in with a chair. The man who raped my mother on the floor while I watched from the crack in the door.

Once I meet the man, I'll know if he is the one. I would recognize him anywhere.

From the look on Damon's face, he knows what my answer will be. Which proves my deal with the devil is inevitable. I will trade anything for revenge.

Even Beatrix Cartwright.

CHAPTER FIFTEEN

THE NICE THING about only working one day a week means that I have most of the week for leisure. Walking the park that winds behind my loft. Painting. Reading. I thought that it was a fulfilling life. A sign of success that my bank account continues to grow through solid investments. And the Saturday nights have always been more about pleasure than work.

Today nothing seems to hold my interest. My books look empty and cold. The outside is a lonely place. This is Bea's fault. The world only looks colorful when she's near me, which is hardly any time at all.

Suddenly one day a week seems like not enough.

I'm looking through my phone, listless, before finally giving in. I pull up the video app so that I can view her page. There are so many videos here. So many days of her. It feels like a feast for someone who's been starving, even though I know it isn't real. Is this what her fans feel like? I scroll down to the comments.

There are many of only a few words: *Beautiful. Queen. Perfect soul.*

Many emojis as well. Hearts and music notes and faces that are crying, with happiness I think.

Other comments are more in-depth. *I love you so much, Bea. I'm your biggest fan and you're beautiful in every way. Follow me back PLS.*

And, *When are you going to go on tour?? I would love to hear you LIVE. #frontrow*

There are also some rather inappropriate ones that have me raising my eyebrows. If they are willing to say this in a public forum, I wonder what kind of private messages she gets. There was no reason for her to hire someone to take her virginity. There's no shortage of volunteers in the comments section.

But I know more than anyone that women don't hire me because there's no one else. They hire me because they want me to be the empty man, the one who can fuck them the way they want, not the way I want, the one who can act like I love them without feeling a thing.

And I'm good at being that man. Empty.

I scroll back to the top, where a new video has been uploaded since I looked at the page yesterday. This one is titled *Over the Rainbow*. I press the PLAY button and settle in to watch.

Most of the videos start with music. Only rarely does she say a brief piece before she begins. This time she begins speaking. "I met someone recently, someone who made me think that maybe there's more to life than what I knew before. Someone who makes me think there's somewhere else worth going."

My heart squeezes, because she must be talking about me. I can hear it in the husky bent of her voice, the way she speaks when my mouth is on her clit. Hungry and low.

"Most people would think he's happy. It feels like he's full of joy, but there's sadness, too. A part of him that longs for a world more colorful than this one."

How does she see inside me, like my skin is made of glass?

"And when I'm around him I long for that world, too. Have you ever met a person like that? A person who made you dream of more?"

There's a silence in which my mind fills in the answer. *You make me dream, Bea.* Because it's not as simple as one direction. It's what happens when we're together, the possibilities like sparks in the air, giving us a glimpse of what could be.

"I love doing the new songs for you, but I have this one on my mind. It's a classic song. I'm sure you've heard it before, but maybe today it will sound new to you like it does to me."

And then she plays the song in a slow, sultry, beautiful tune. It makes goose bumps rise on my arms, the deep sound of her breath coming through the small speakers. How does she do this?

By the time she gets to the end, there are tears in my eyes. I do not have the worry that other men have in Tanglewood. That other men had in Tangier, also. That I will not be properly masculine if I cry, but there is very little that can move me. A beautiful painting. A poem. I can enjoy them without being moved, but this is different. It's like she's singing to me, and my body responds as if she's touching me. I want to clench my hand in her wild hair. I want to press my lips against the rapid pulse at the base of her throat. God, she's perfect.

The notes end in a weighted silence. And then the video ends.

I feel the loss of her, acute and painful.

The video app gives me only a small pause before spinning into another one of her videos. And another, while I sit there, cold as a statue on top of a building, watching the city stream by.

Eventually the app moves to play other musicians who share their work. And then pop music published by the major labels.

Still, I cannot bring myself to move.

The notes she played have embedded themselves in my head. It's all I can hear.

Until the phone buzzes in my hand. An incoming text. I glance down, detached from this ordinary world, disinterested, until I see Melissande's name. I try to ignore how much anticipation rises within me at the thought of seeing Bea again.

She booked the next three weeks.

A deep breath makes me realize I had been holding it, but for how long? Since I saw Bea perform that haunting melody? Or longer, since I left her bed? I text back, *Okay,* glad Melissande isn't here to see me. She would sense that something was wrong, no matter how well I try to hide it.

Your other clients will lose their minds.

My other clients will go back to their regular lives. They will find a nice man in a bar. Or finally approach someone they've had a crush on. There's nothing for them with me.

It's Melissande who's in danger of losing her mind. *I'm not giving you any more nights,* I type.

Three dots hover on the screen for a long time. Either Melissande is typing out something very long or she's doing a lot of erasing and starting over. In the end her message is brief: *I made you.*

That makes me laugh out loud, the sound echoing in the large loft. *Do you want me to thank you?* I type back, before adding, *Thank you, Melissande. For making me a whore.*

She'll read the sarcasm fine, because it's been a very long time since we were friends. A very long time since we were lovers. There must be fondness there, to make me reluctant to ruin her. I'm not in the business of ruining women. Usually I prefer to pleasure them. Could I make an exception for Damon Scott? Would I make an exception for revenge?

It is perhaps ominous that I don't know the answer myself.

Chapter Sixteen

I N MY LOFT I prepare a gourmet picnic with sliced meats and creamy cheeses. There are plump grapes and ripe strawberries. A baguette from the French bakery so fresh it crackles when I place it in the bag. Most of these items are easy to prepare. The only thing I make from scratch is a moist brioche with hints of orange and white chocolate, soft on the inside, the sugar caramelized on the outside. My mother taught me to make this.

She worked twelve hours a day in a hotel that cost more per night than she earned in a month. She did not have money for luxury or time for hobbies. But in the few minutes she had between waking and work, she loved to cook. Recipes handed down from her mother but spiced with what was available in the open-air markets of Tangier. There was ratatouille made with tomatoes and zucchini and bay leaf, but also couscous and ginger. French lentils with fava beans and cumin. She loved to try new things, both of us tasting from the pot while the meal simmered, heating the small room we shared.

I don't have her level of curiosity or wonder about cooking, but every meal I prepare is an homage to her. If you would have asked me if I loved my mother, I would have said yes. But I spent too much time fighting in the streets to be what you'd call a good son.

She was the one who let me out of the closet, limping and bleeding and crying too hard to speak. Even then I knew that the police would not help us against a rich American tourist. I cooked every day for her for a week, before she was well enough to return to work.

We did not speak of what happened that night. She didn't wish to, and I was too angry. Too selfish. Too busy fighting in the streets, thinking I would make something of myself in a city that hardly recognized me as human. But somewhere in my chest was the certainty that I would find that man.

After the cancer took her, it became my only purpose.

So when I met beautiful Melissande, when I found out where she came from—I knew she would be the way to revenge. She offered me the chance to come with her. It seemed almost miraculous, that I had fallen in love with a woman and could achieve my goal at the same time.

She kept me in a state of ignorant bliss in her bed for a year before revealing my purpose in Tanglewood. I would be a prostitute, catering to the wealthy men and women of society who wanted a dark-haired fallen angel in their beds. Someone with an exotic accent and very little inhibition.

That's when I learned that I could not have love and revenge.

There could only be one or the other.

My mind is in turmoil as the brioche cools on the oven, but I move with determination as I pack them with the rest of the picnic. We won't need Bea's tiny kitchen tonight, though I still hope to dine with her. The drive to the hotel is done in silence, without the usual joy I feel when driving the Bugatti.

I feel only a small amount of guilt for using my key card without being invited. It only takes me to the entrance. Once inside I knock on the wall and wait, a strange fluttering of nerves.

What if Bea isn't here? What if she *is* here but she doesn't want to see me? She isn't paying for tonight. There's nothing on the books with Melissande until tomorrow—our standing Saturday appointment.

From the elevator car I can see the empty living room. Soft voices filter through the closed bedroom door. "Hello? Is anyone home?"

The door opens, revealing a young woman with blonde hair with pink streaks. "Uh. Hi?"

Not Bea. For a moment I'm so thrown I wonder if I somehow found the wrong building. A different gaudy hotel established by the ex-owner of a French brothel. A different penthouse with an agoraphobic little ex-virgin. "Is Beatrix here?"

"Bea," the blonde says in a singsong voice. "Have you been holding out on me?"

Her voice comes from deep within the penthouse. "What?"

"There's a young Cary Grant at your door, so either L'Etoile has seriously upped their staffing game or you have been keeping very big, very sexy secrets." The young woman winks at me.

"Is there a baguette in that basket or are you just happy to see me?"

I laugh, as comfortable with flirting as she is. "Both, *naturellement.*"

"A man to please all appetites," she says as Bea peeks around the corner, hair even more wild and dangerous than usual. It's untamable, that hair. Like the woman.

"Oh," she says, though it's more like a squeak. "Did we have an…"

Appointment, she means to say. "A date? But no, I wished to surprise you."

"You did surprise me." Her gaze slides to her friend, who's watching us with undisguised pleasure and interest. "Harper, this is… Hugo. And, Hugo…"

"Harper," I say with my best smile, which produces a blush. I recognize her faintly from the society papers, this girl who is related to Christopher from the Thieves Club. The stepsister that makes him scowl every time he says something about her.

"Ohhh my," Harper says. "Do you just go around smiling on the street, making people fall over and having cars crash around you? It's dangerous."

"*Non*, this one I reserve for private company." I turn to Bea, who looks torn. She's biting her lip, leaving indents in the plump flesh. Everything about her calls to me, but it's almost a relief that she's turning me away. I shouldn't be using her for information, shouldn't be trying to get close to her to find out more about the man who owns this hotel. "I can come back another time. You are clearly having a girls' night, and I'm the intruder."

I hid my disappointment rather well, I thought, but Bea still looks crestfallen. Crestfallen and beautiful in a black lace blouse that flutters around her elegant neck and jeans—a more casual look than she's ever worn for our dates. "Wait."

"I'm so out of here," Harper says, pointing a finger at me. "And I'm going to drag the details out of Bea, so you better make them worth our while. Dirty. Salacious. Shocking."

"I do aim to please," I say, my smile lazy. Of course I would love for the night to be dirty, but that depends on quite a lot. Like whether Bea will even speak to me after crashing her night.

It only takes a moment for Harper to grab her things—a model of phone that isn't available commercially yet and a handbag shaped like a panda. Then she leaves down the elevator, making promises to call Bea the next day.

As soon as we're alone, Bea shakes her head, her smile both exasperated and fond. "She's never going to let up asking questions about you now."

"I'm sure we can give you plenty to tell. That is, if you wish to spend the evening with me."

"Of course I do." She pauses as if to check herself. "But I didn't book this time with the agency. I thought you were coming tomorrow."

"This isn't through the agency," I say lightly, to pretend it's no big deal.

Of course it's a huge deal. When was the last time I spent a night with a woman without being paid for it? The thought would disturb me, if I didn't have an ulterior motive for being here. It's not quite as much distance as money, but it's enough to keep this from meaning too much.

She looks at me, skeptical, uncertain. "So this is… what?"

"Why does a man spend time with a beautiful woman? It's a date, if you'll give me the honor. That's what this is."

I am not so worried about deceiving her, or at least, this is what I tell myself. She may not have paid for this night, but she understands the nature of this relationship. And soon enough, once she's gotten over her initial nervousness about sex, she will move on to a man more appropriate for her. Maybe one who will finally help her leave this tower prison of hers. I will merely be a distant memory to make her embarrassed.

Her green eyes are deep tonight, without the usual walls that keep her hidden. I can see her fear and her excitement. She looks impossibly innocent like this. "Do you want to come in?" she asks, a little shy.

"*Non.* I wish to take you outside."

Dismay. "You know I can't."

I make a noncommittal hum in my throat. "Whether you can or you can't, I won't ask you to set even one foot off the property. At least not tonight."

"Really?"

"But of course."

She narrows her eyes. "You know, it doesn't escape my notice that you're carrying a picnic basket. Where are you planning to spread that out? The lobby?"

All she gets is a half smile. "You will have to trust me for that."

"Trust you?" she asks, so incredulous it would wound me if I didn't know how deeply her fear of the outside runs. She doesn't trust anyone.

"You trust me with your body," I remind her. "With your most private places. With your pleasure. I'm only asking for a little bit more, *mon amie.* Trust me with tonight."

She takes a shuddering breath, which flutters the lace at her throat. "Okay."

It moves me more than it should, her trust in me. Silently, urgently, I swear to myself that I won't betray that trust. She may never know my true interest in L'Etoile, but my feelings about her are pure. I like her. I respect her. And I will do

145

nothing to make her doubt those things.

It takes only a little coaxing to bring her into the elevator.

Only when I press the UP button does she start to breathe faster. "What are you doing?"

"Taking us to the roof. There's a beautiful garden up there. I've seen it through Google Maps. And you have exclusive access to it. I'm shocked you don't spend all your time there."

"That's not...part of the...hotel." She's breathing faster now, close to panic.

I take her face between my hands, both gentle and firm. "It is part of the hotel. The same structure where you spend all of your time. You do not have to leave to see the stars."

"That's what windows are for."

My laugh comes out, surprised, unexpected. "*Non.*"

"We can spread out the picnic on the carpet. It will be fun."

"Perhaps another time. Tonight we will dine in the night air, and you will be fine."

She searches my eyes. "What if I'm not?"

Trust. That's what she's giving me right now, and the gift is worth more than a thousand nights. "I'll be with you every second, Bea. I won't let anything happen to you."

CHAPTER SEVENTEEN

FROM THE AERIAL view on my computer I saw the small greenhouse full of lush plants. The elaborate black iron table and chairs for dining. The expanse of wooden deck and brick walls. It's a beautiful space, meant to be enjoyed, meant to be lived in. The only person who comes up here is the caretaker. Not Bea, even though she's the only occupant of L'Etoile allowed to use the space.

The elevator doors begin to close behind me. I put my hand out to stop them. Bea looks at me with wide, unblinking eyes. Like a rabbit, I think. Too afraid to run away.

"Come here," I murmur.

A jerky shake of her head. "Can't," she says between gritted teeth.

"What will happen if you come?"

"I don't know." Her gaze darts behind me. The view is peaceful, but her expression is full of turmoil. Violence, even. The certainty is a blow to my stomach, making every muscle in my body clench. Because of what happened to her parents. Such a strange and random thing, to be killed by pirates.

And yet it wasn't random at all. They were targeted because of their wealth.

Which means she could be a target, too. No wonder she does not step foot outside. It's a wonder that she let me through the door that first night. My dismay only strengthens my decision to help.

"I imagine that if I tell you nothing will happen, you won't believe me."

Her eyes plead with me, beautiful and haunted. "I do believe you, with my head. It's my body that doesn't seem to understand. It doesn't even let me come outside. I'm stuck here."

She means that she's rooted to the spot in the elevator, but it's more than that. She's stuck in this old hotel. Stuck in a life she was never meant to lead. Her parents were tech moguls and famous concert pianists. Their gifts should have been a privilege for Bea. Instead it's trapped her.

"What does your therapist say?" I don't wish to damage her, despite my own certainty that she needs to leave this place, that it's imperative for her. Life or death.

"I don't see her anymore."

"Why not?"

She mumbles at the marble floor of the elevator. "She wanted me to leave." Then she meets my gaze, almost angry. "She didn't understand. You don't, either."

"Explain it to me."

"I mean, I *really* can't move. Physically. My body won't let me."

I cock my head, examining her the same way I looked at Minette huddled behind the dresser, needing me to take her out. "What if I move you?"

She shakes her head miserably. "I'll just freak out. Screaming. Crying. I've tried that before."

With who? I want to know who she trusted enough to take her outside, even if it failed. The same person who put her here in the first place? "If you scream, if you cry, I'll bring you back inside."

"You make it sound easy."

"Not easy." No one looking at her, the strain around her eyes, the tension in her body, could think this would be easy. "But you're strong enough to do it. With me, Bea."

I set down the picnic basket so that my hands are free. Then I move so that I'm facing her, my foot still blocking the door from closing. She stands in front of me, inside the elevator that she must have taken hundreds of times. Thousands of times. She knows this elevator too well, while a single step outside feels like a wild jump across oceans.

Her lower lip trembles, and I lean my head close, waiting for her to jerk back. There's every chance this won't work, that we'll end up having the picnic spread out on her bed.

She holds still as my lips press against hers, and I'm suspended in that moment. *Stuck*, that's the word she used. I'm not stuck, though. I'm floating. Free.

Our breaths come together, her skin flushed and fragrant.

Her hands are in mine. I could pull her out— one inch, two. I could carry her over this threshold, but I wasn't lying when I said she was strong enough. Strong enough to make the step herself.

A small swipe of my tongue over her bottom lip.

Then I move back, leaving only a moment between us. She sways toward me, wanting more. I surrender to her for a second, this time a kiss to the corner of her mouth. And then retreat again.

She comes closer, leaning toward me, her feet

in the elevator.

"Bea," I say, gaze dark on hers. In my eyes I let her see every ounce of desire I have for her, which is more than I really should. It makes me naked, this look, more than if I stripped down to nothing.

Her lips part the slightest amount—an acknowledgment. A plea.

The kiss that follows is clumsy as she steps forward onto the hard wood, almost falling into my arms, caught by me, making a little panicked, pleased sound in my mouth.

Ding. The elevator doors close behind her.

I realize that I can't use her. Not tonight, anyway.

It means too much, that she would trust me this way. And so I hold her, safe and willing in my arms. Perhaps she feels the change in me, because she relaxes into my body.

Chapter Eighteen

WE FEAST ON cheeses and fruit, not quite acknowledging the buildings that peak around us like mountains. She trusted me enough to stay on the roof, and for now that will be enough.

The sun sets in a glory of golden blue while she sips champagne, her gaze studiously on my own. I fill my own glass and take a drink, because I need the courage more than her. She's already the bravest woman I know. I'm the one wondering how I care about her so much after so little time. Wondering what I'll do when she's done with me.

I may have decided not to use her for revenge, tonight, but that does not mean I'll ask no questions. In fact I'm brimming with questions. Running over with them. I set the glass down carefully, wondering how much to ask. Needing to know the answers.

"Will you tell me now why you wanted to lose

your virginity in this way? I know there's more you aren't telling me. More than loneliness." I suspected that from the very first night, a secret motivation that drives her, something close to desperation. It would have stopped a moral man from touching her.

Unfortunately for her I gave up any semblance of morality long ago.

She sighs, looking out at the city. Has she ever seen it without a panel of glass blocking it? A cool wind touches my skin. It gives her hair a sense of ceaseless motion, as if it's alive. "There is a reason. I mean, I was curious. I've always been curious, but when I turned twenty…"

At her pause I force myself to stay silent. This is her story; I have to let her tell it. But I do take her hand in mine, because that's what I'm here for, isn't it? My body and the comfort it can bring. It's all I have to offer.

Her hand squeezes back. "Someone proposed to me."

Shock tightens my stomach, though I don't know why I should be surprised. She's a beautiful, smart, extremely desirable young woman. Even trapped in her castle, she has suitors. There's a churning inside me, a strange mixture of jealousy and loss. *She was never mine.*

"What was your answer?" I'm pleased that my tone comes out light.

"I said I'd think about it, but I don't want to marry him."

Worry furrows her expression, and I feel myself grow hot from anger. "Are you afraid to tell him no?"

If there is someone threatening her, I have no problem standing up to this faceless, nameless asshole. I may live a life of ease and luxury these days, in high-rise hotels and satin sheets, but I was a street mongrel once. I fought and scraped and clawed my way through Tangier's back alleys. A rich frat boy in Tanglewood will not stand a chance.

She looks away with a slight shake of her head, not quite agreeing but not refuting it either. "This is going to sound weird, but I had this feeling that he only wanted me because…"

The final piece falls into place, making acid rise in my throat. "Because you're a virgin."

"I mean, he didn't *say* that, but it felt like that was part of the reason. There's never been anything romantic between us. He's been with lots of women in the papers. So why would he propose to me unless there was something different about me."

There are many different things about Beatrix Cartwright, and they have nothing to do with the hymen that I took from her. But I do not point that out. If she doubts the motives of this man, then he is not worthy of her. "Have you told him that you are no longer a virgin?"

If he wanted her innocence, he might become angry when she tells him.

She seems to sense my concern. "He wouldn't hurt me."

"Then why not simply tell him no?"

"Our relationship is... complicated. I didn't want to hurt his feelings."

A sudden suspicion makes my blood pressure spike. "This man who proposed. Is he perhaps the same person who became your guardian when you were a child?"

She looks stricken. "How do you know about that?"

I force myself not to growl in frustration. "Someone must have done so. You were under-age."

"Yes, he was my dad's business partner. And he became my guardian."

"And he wants to *marry* you?" This time I do not manage to sound light or calm. I'm furious.

"It's not like we were ever close. He didn't

become a parent to me. He was more like… the money person. He was the custodian of my trust. And he made sure I had everything I needed."

If he had really done that, Bea would be able to leave this hotel. "He must be older than you."

A miserable shrug. "I suppose. That's not the reason I don't want to marry him, though. I just don't love him, you know? Not even as a guardian, really. And definitely not as a husband."

It's almost impossible to control my breathing. I'm like a bull, snorting and pawing at the ground. The image of anyone hurting Bea, coercing her, making her feel small—the red cape. "You don't need a reason to tell him no."

"I know that I can say no. That I *should* say no, but I think… once he finds out I'm not a virgin anymore, he'll lose interest. And that will be easier. That's why I called the service that first night. Why I wanted sex without the pleasure."

My stomach drops. "Who owns the penthouse suite, Bea?"

"He owns the hotel."

"So you have to marry him or he'll kick you out?" For any other heiress that wouldn't be a hardship, but for a scared young woman with anxiety and agoraphobia? Yes, that's a sufficient threat.

My blood runs hot because only a bastard would give her that choice.

"He didn't say that," she says, defensive.

"But you're worried that would happen."

"I'd rather avoid the problem."

And that sums up the reason she's still in the penthouse, why the biggest step she's taken in ten years is onto this rooftop. Because she wants to avoid fear instead of facing it. In some ways she's incredibly strong—the music she makes, the empire she's built from it.

Even hiring me, a stranger, to do intimate things with her, fighting years of isolation, took a strength most people don't have. In other ways she's still a scared little girl, trapped by her grief.

I brush the backs of my fingers against her cheek, pushing aside the idea of this man trying to marry Bea, letting go for a few blissful moments the idea of revenge. Ignoring the knowledge that at some point, I'll be the problem Bea wants to avoid. Dread forms knots in my stomach, but it can't touch the immediacy of feeling her skin against mine.

She turns her face, pressing a kiss against my knuckles.

"Here?" I ask softly, giving her the option to retreat. It's the better part of valor, after all, and she's shown plenty of valor tonight. Being here on the roof is a new place to her, even if it's technically part of the building she's called home for over a decade.

She does not look away from my eyes, her green ones dark as emeralds in the final glory of dusk. "Something to remember this night."

Even she can feel the sands of time slipping away.

I lean close to her, pressing a kiss to the constellations across the bridge of her nose. Her eyes are closed, so I kiss one eyelid and then the other. She blows out a soft breath, still not looking at me but *feeling* me. She's so attuned to me in this moment that she knows when my gaze lowers to her mouth. Her lips part, and I make her wait. Cruel, this. I make her wait while I study those plush pink lips. There's even the faintest spray of freckles over her lips.

When I kiss her, I imagine I can taste them, these stars. They taste like woman and salt and something elemental to the universe, as if I'm taking sustenance from her. Nourishing myself with her flavor.

"Look up, Bea."

She looks at me, and that should be gratifying to me. It's not quite an accident that I ended up in a profession that amounts to exhibitionism with a different woman every night. They like to look at me, and I enjoy being looked at. But I want something different for her. Something better.

"Up," I say, giving her a tap on the chin.

Obediently her lashes lift. She looks up at the stars and lets out a shuddery breath. "How do people do this every day? They walk outside and they don't even worry? It seems impossible."

"You do things that are impossible," I tell her, tracing a finger lazily down her jaw. "You make beautiful music that millions of people want to watch."

And you make me dream of a different life than this.

Her eyes become wet with tears, but she does not look away from the dark sky. "Anything could happen. We're not protected out here."

And then despite my best efforts I cannot help but to think of her. Of my mother who could not even find safety in the small rooms we rented. "Safety isn't real, Bea. It's a dream."

A tear runs down her cheek. "Why would you say that?"

"I'm sorry," I say, immediately contrite. That isn't for her. That's only for me, the sense that I will never be safe, that I will never be enough. That I can never make up for being a scared little boy in the closet.

She shakes her head. "No, don't be. You're right. Oh God, you're right."

I can't convey to her all I wish to say—that she should be free, that she should be mine. Only one of those will come true. "No, I was foolish. But of course safety is real."

Except that I'm lying, and we both know it. Safety is a dream that only children have. Both of us grew up too soon, aware that everything we knew before would never come true.

Her eyes are as wide and as mysterious as the universe itself. She is a galaxy and a black hole, creation and destruction in one female-shaped body. "Dream with me," she says.

That's the only invitation I need. I lay her back on the picnic blanket, resting her head on my folded-up jacket. Unveiling her body to the moonlight has a sense of rightness, as if I've been waiting all my life to see her pale curves made luminescent, as if she's been waiting forever to be bared.

Sailors used the night sky to guide their path. That's what I become this night, finding my way over the slope of her breast to the tight point of her nipple, following down the flat of her stomach. They are signposts along the way, but my direction is the North Star. For this I must spread her legs, push her thighs apart and part the copper-colored curls.

The feel of her clit against my tongue is almost enough to burn. Too bright for mere mortals. I curl myself around her, letting her feel my desire, my devotion. She's the one who moves first, finding friction against my tongue. *Yes, mon amie. Take what you need. Fuck me.*

I don't have to say the words, because she's finding freedom underneath the stars. Finding safety in this shared dream, where she can rock her hips against my face, pulling her own orgasm to the surface.

Two fingers slide in easily. It's a little harder to fit the third, because she's still tight. Still untried, so I move her softly—easy, easy. I twist my fingers inside her to the same rhythm she's given me, because she is the one playing me. I may have arrived with my bedroom tricks and my sexual experience, but they were only an ordinary song. She's the one who turned it into something new, something beautiful. Something uniquely her own, the way she does at the piano every day.

She comes with a wild sound at the sky, her

head thrown back.

There's something animalistic about her like this, naked and primal. It calls to something primal in me, and I tear off my clothes with an urgency that causes the bespoke shirt to rip. And I don't fucking care. All I need is to feel her against me, around me, underneath me. Nothing else matters.

I mount her with a need unlike anything I've ever known, barely tugging on a condom before I press inside her, expecting to find relief, surcease in the wet heat of her pussy. It only drives me higher, the swollen pressure, only makes me need more, feeling her dampness at the base of my cock.

She doesn't watch the night sky anymore. She's looking into my eyes, but her expression holds the same wonder, the same wariness. What does she see inside me? There's a vast emptiness there, too. Only she has the stars. Only with her is there ever any light.

"Once more," I tell her. "Come again, so I can feel you on my cock. That's how I want to come, Bea. Against my will, with your beautiful body forcing it out of me."

Her eyelids lower. "Make me."

So I angle her hips to receive my thrust in the

right place and then drive home. It only takes a single thrust before she's panting, squealing, squirming to get away. It's too acute, this kind of pleasure, but the challenge can only be answered this way. Again and again. I fuck her until she comes with an almost guttural sound, grasping at my shoulders, clawing at them as if we'll never get close enough.

The pain would be enough to wake me from a dream, so I relish the red marks she leaves on my skin, proof that I must be awake even as an orgasm rips through me like a shooting star, too fierce to be contained by my skin, rushing out of me like a thousand fiery sparks. I convulse over Bea's body, collapsing onto her because she's the only relief I've found in a wide-open universe, the only light in a too-dark sky.

Chapter Nineteen

W E'RE SPREAD OUT on the seat cushions, which are the only things separating us from cool, hard concrete. That and the dubious protection of my jacket as a blanket, but I've never been warmer. The residual heat between us simmers in the air. Bea rests her head on my arm, looking up at the stars. They're beautiful, I know. Luminous and ever expanding, but I can't take my eyes off her profile. The faint constellations of her freckles glow a thousand times more.

Without the physical sensation the dread rushes back, gnawing and fierce. The realization that we have very little time left. Maybe only tonight. My hands tighten instinctively around Bea before I can catch myself. I release her right away, pretending to run my hands down her arms, but she looks back at me with too much awareness.

"Is it difficult?" she asks, so soft I almost don't hear. "Doing this?"

My standard answer would be something charming and glib. Of course I do not mind having sex. It's the easiest job in the world. Something keeps me from giving her pretend, because it's not always easy. The sex is good, but the facade... it wears on me. Having to be someone else.

I don't want to do that with her. "Sometimes."

Her fingers draw lazy circles on my chest. "If you aren't attracted to a woman?"

"That's rarely a problem. I love women. Their bodies. Their hearts. Their minds. The way they're so wrapped up in saving the world that it almost hurts them to focus on their own pleasure."

She looks skeptical. "There's never a woman you don't want to..."

"There's not much honor in my profession," I try to explain. "But if there's one part... a woman who doesn't feel beautiful. One who isn't attractive, according to what society tells her. Showing her that she deserves to be cherished is something worth doing."

"Is that what I am to you?" she asks. "A charity case?"

There's a wild thump in my heart. Surprise.

"*Non.*"

"What am I then?"

"You're a gift."

Bea rests her chin on my shoulder, watching me with too much knowledge. "What about you?"

"I do feel beautiful," I say blandly, a small attempt at humor.

She gives me a shy smile. "You deserve to be cherished."

My stomach clenches, hard enough that I'm afraid the baguette and brie will make a swift return. It's no secret that women want me for the way I look, for the way I make them feel. No one wants what's inside. There's nothing here. A hollow space where a person might be.

I look up at the stars, counting them, distracting myself from the earnest woman, warm and willing in my arms. As if I won't dream of this later.

The tickle of her hair is my only warning. Her lips are warm and lush against my chest. Every muscle in my body tenses as she places another kiss, this one an inch lower. My cock does not mind that it has just been spent; by the third kiss it's already hard again.

Her lips are heaven alone, but the brush of

skin as she moves over me drives me insane. The whisper of hair over my body makes me mad. "God," I groan. "What are you doing?"

"Can't you tell?"

She's halfway down the plane of my stomach, working across the ridges of my abs with clear appreciation. My cock flexes as if anticipating where she'll go next.

Down, down, down.

"You can't—" I'm panting now, almost incoherent. "You don't have to—"

Her smile is devilish, almost enough to make me come from the inherent feminine power within. "What did you tell me? It's rather embarrassing how much I want to."

My breath hitches. "Bea."

"But only with your permission."

This will be more than a blowjob. That much I know, because I want her more than air. I'm already moved by her belief in me. Humbled that she would give me her virginity, in every way. There won't be any recovering from her after this. "Please."

Before I've finished speaking the word, her lips touch me. She tastes me with an innocence that makes me harder, the peach blush of her lips impossibly pale against the dark red arousal at my crown. First there is only a kiss, far too quick, the way you would buss someone on the cheek. Friendly but impersonal. She comes in again for a longer press, this one testing, unsure.

Only then does her tongue dart out, a small swipe that makes my hips jerk.

"Like that?" she asks, but she already knows. Her eyes sparkle with mischief.

"Devil woman," I say, cursing her in every language until her mouth returns. Her lips circle the head, and I lose all sense of words. There's only sensation—hot, wet, deep. An ocean so wide and dark that I would drown here. I never want to leave.

She is clumsy at first, which only serves to emphasize the gift she gives me. The way her tongue explores me, darting and quick. The way she takes too much inside, her eyes going wide. I push her back gently, stroking her hair. "Go slow, *mon amie*. Be careful."

Someone must be careful with her, because I cannot. I'm reckless with her, this fragile flower, made of sunshine in a bottle. I'm spilling her everywhere.

It does not matter that she has no practiced moves to make me come. I'm close, from seeing her taste me, from feeling her mouth and her passion.

Except... *there.*

She touches her tongue against a certain spot, and my eyes roll back. *God,* that was close. I almost came in her mouth, without warning, like the most crude sort of man. It must have been an accident.

And then she does it again.

My hips thrust into her mouth without permission from me. "*Mon Dieu,*" I mutter, panting, unable to see anything except stars.

When my eyes focus again, I see her watching me. That's how she's doing this. Because she's watching me, gauging every reaction, weighing every touch. Figuring out what I like best, because she thinks I deserve to be cherished.

Desperation fills my chest, because eventually she'll find out the truth. I'm not worthy of her mouth, her body. I'm not worthy of anything.

She touches that place beneath my cock for a third time, and I lose control. Her hair is grasping me, or I'm grasping her hair, pulling her close. Pressure bursts from the base of my spine, turning every muscle in my body to pulsing stone. My mouth opens on a silent cry, the only sound a guttural surrender as my cock empties down her throat.

There's no reason for her to stay within my grasp, to let me pull at her and thrust into her mouth two more times, wringing out the most intense orgasm of my life. This is a base act, almost cruel the way I use her. I can't hate myself for it, because I would do it again.

She sits up, wiping her thumb across her bottom lip, looking both pleased with herself and self-conscious. "Was that okay?"

At this exact second I'm struggling to move my limbs or form words. It feels like a Herculean effort, putting together a complete sentence. "That was incredible. Come here."

I don't wait for her to snuggle in but instead pull her down, rolling on top of her with a burst of gratitude. My hand slides down her body, reveling in the way she twists and turns into my touch. Her body is wet and swollen, made ready for me.

The blowjob turned her on. That knowledge sits inside me, too powerful to resist. I slip my fingers inside, my thumb rough on her clit. I stroke her once, twice, three times. She comes with a soft exhalation, her body turning pliant, eyelids heavy as she sinks into sleep.

Chapter Twenty

THROUGH THE WALLS I can hear the soccer games that Mr. Alami watches every night. From somewhere a baby cries. The windows don't close all the way. It smells like the smoke from the hookah lounge down the street. Our building is never quiet, never asleep, but no one came when Mama let out a short, surprised scream. They didn't come when I yelled at the man hurting her or when he hit me.

He's gone now. The bed stopped making that horrible creak. From the crack in the closet door I watched his shadow stand up and fix his clothes before he walked out the front door.

Mama's shadow got up much slower.

I can tell she's in pain by the way she's hunched over, by the sniffles she probably thinks I can't hear. She doesn't come and move the chair locking me inside. Does she not know I'm here? Did she forget? I stay silent, my arms wrapped around my knees. I can tell my eye is getting big and swollen where he hit me, but it doesn't hurt. It doesn't feel like anything.

There's a high-pitched sound that I recognize as the pipes that are behind this wall. The shower is running, with its leaky spray and its hot water that runs out. *Mama.*

It feels like forever when she finally comes and lets me out.

I run to her, pressing my face against her warmth, her dress clean and soft—not the stiff uniform she wore home from the hotel, smelling of sharp chemicals, the one she wore when *he* came. *We have to call the police*, I tell her in French, my words too fast and too afraid.

She shakes her head, slow and sure. "*Non.* We call no one."

I have grown up for seven years on these streets. No one trusts the police, but this is something very bad. This is what they are supposed to protect us against. "He hurt you."

There is no mark on her eye. It was not that kind of hurt. "He's a powerful man. Very rich. Staying at the hotel in the top floor. The penthouse."

He may be very rich in the top floor, the penthouse, but he came into our rooms. "So he can do that and nothing happens to him?"

She looks away, hiding the tears. "Don't, Hugo."

Or maybe she's looking away because she does not want to see my tears. "You are wrong," I tell her, even though I'm afraid she's right. Rich men and women can do anything they want.

The sheets on the bed are still rumpled, the pillows fallen off. It's her bed, but I have crawled in at night to cuddle with her, when my cot in the main room feels too cold and sad. There's only one bedroom, and it has never bothered me, never felt too small or too poor until now.

On the floor there's something brown and flat. Something that does not belong.

I pick it up, feeling the very smooth material. Inside there is scribbled writing I can't read. And money. So much money.

Mama gasps, "What is that?"

She knows what it is.

I know how to pick pockets. This one would be a prize, but tonight I'm not interested in the pink and green slips of paper. I'm looking for something with a picture on it. A name.

There is nothing except for a matchbox with a design on it, like stars.

And the letters L'ETOILE.

Mama takes the wallet from me, very quick,

the way she would do if I had taken something I shouldn't, if I had done something wrong. "We have to give it back."

"At least keep the money." I don't know what we will do with the money. Buy food or a better lock for the door. Maybe a knife so I can stop another man who tries this.

Her eyes become dark. "I do not want his money. I'm not a *kahba*."

For the most part Mama speaks French or the English she learned working at the hotel. That word is Arabic. It means the girls who stand on the streets. The ones who visit the lounge late at night and leave with American men. They would get to keep the money.

That's what I learn that night.

CHAPTER TWENTY-ONE

I WAKE UP with a racing heart, as if something has gone terribly wrong.

Vaguely I remember the dream. The night I wish I could forget. The image of L'Etoile's logo stamped into my brain. Decades later, and I still have the same fucking nightmare.

A sound comes to me, keening that makes the hair on my neck rise. Heavy shadows in the past keep me in the dark longer than I should be. I blink against the too-bright moon, struggling to remember where I am. Hands are grasping at my arm. An urgency pounds in my skull, too hard and too fast.

"Oh my God, oh my God, oh my God."

The words filter through my blurry consciousness, making me snap to alertness. Beatrix. And she sounds like she did last night, afraid and trembling, only much worse.

My heart clenches when I look down at the sight of her. She's curled up into a ball, clinging onto my arm like it's a life raft in a wild ocean. Her wild hair sticks to the side of her face, her skin slick with sweat. "Oh my God," she whispers, her eyes squeezed shut.

"Bea, I'm here. I'm right here."

"It's not enough."

The words hit me like a ton of bricks, because of course it's not enough. I would never be enough. "I'll take you inside. Can you stand?"

We're only a few yards away from the elevator. The dining area and large concrete pots with plants in them block our path. She shakes her head, burying her head against me.

I would rather convince her to come with me, but her whole body shakes violently. Small sounds of distress are coming from her, as if she doesn't even register I'm here. I need to get her out of this situation and back where she feels safe—the penthouse.

She whimpers. "Hugo?"

Crouching over her, one hand on her arm, the other resting lightly on her head, I have never felt more helpless. This woman is suffering. It doesn't matter whether it's a physical punch in the stomach; it's clear she's hurt. And it's my fault. I'm the one who brought her here. "I'm going to carry you inside."

Her body relaxes only a fraction, but I'm in tune with her enough to feel it.

Which is also why my body is tied up in knots, my usual calm gone, any ability to seduce or reason with her disappeared into the early dawn. Anxiety clenches hard around my throat, as if we're connected, part of the same body.

That's how it feels when I lift her in my arms, when she curls herself into me—like I can finally take a breath. Her hair tickles my nose, curls itself around my face. It makes me pull her closer.

I press a kiss to her head, already striding toward the elevator. "Almost there, sweetheart."

"Sorry," she whispers. "Sorry. Sorry."

She's apologizing to me? *Mon Dieu.* "There's nothing to be sorry about."

The elevator takes approximately twelve years to make its way up, even though it's private for the penthouse suite. When the doors finally open I step inside and press the P button to return to her suite. We are now indoors, in a place that she's been herself many times, but she does not relax. Instead she clings to me even harder, her arms tight around my neck, her hands clenched in my wrinkled shirt, as if these familiar places have become new and scary.

"Almost there," I murmur on the twenty-four-hour ride down one floor.

The doors slide open, revealing the penthouse suite…that is full of people.

I recognize some of them as hotel staff. The head of concierge. Jessica from the front desk. A maid. And a man in a suit, directing them all with an angry and authoritative voice.

"Where are the police?" he demands, before turning toward us.

For a moment we stand there facing each other, this man who must control Bea's life. The one who's kept her in this tower, whether she sees it that way or not.

"Leave," he says to everyone else without breaking eye contact with me.

The room immediately clears, hotel staff filing past me and leaving the way they came, silent and obedient. Meanwhile I move deeper into the room. Past the stranger, to the bedroom. It's hard to let go of Bea's trembling body, but I lay her down on her rumpled sheets. This is where she should have been sleeping. Where she should have woken up, so that her body wouldn't be flushed and trembling.

"Don't go," she whimpers, grasping my arm.

"But no," I manage to say lightly. "I'm not going anywhere."

Her eyes meet mine, almost glazed from the terror she felt being on the roof. There's pleading in her eyes, whether because she still wishes to apologize or because she's worried I'll abandon her like this.

"Who are you?" a voice asks coldly.

Without letting go of Bea's hand, I turn to face the man in the suit. Only now, with Bea safely tucked in a place familiar to her, can I consider what I know. I thought I would know him immediately, on sight, this man from my nightmare. It seemed clear to me that I would, but now that I look at him I'm not sure.

The man in my dreams is ten feet tall with large muscles. He has a smile that's terrifying, but those are the imaginings of a scared little boy. Now that I'm a man, this one looks ordinary.

Is it him? Or is it merely some other rich asshole with ties to this hotel?

"I'm Bea's lover," I tell him, because I want him angry. Well, he's already angry. I want him frothing and helpless, the way I feel right now, unable to help the woman I care about.

"You're lying," the man says, his lip curled. "She doesn't have a boyfriend."

"Boyfriend? *Non.* I am her lover. Surely you understand the difference."

He snarls in a way that is almost, *almost* familiar. But his hair is peppered with white, his stance leaner than I remember. *Is it him?* "I don't know what kind of scam you think you're running, but this girl is under my protection."

"This *woman* does not need protection against me."

"I'll be the judge of that."

"Stop!" Bea is sitting up in bed, but only barely, holding up a hand as if to ward us both away. My heart breaks for her, that she needs to worry about this when she should be focused on herself. "Please, don't fight. Edward, what are you doing here?"

"Looking for you," he says, taking a step forward which I block with my body. He isn't getting near when she's in this state. He gives me a dark look but stays on his side of the bedroom. "Maria came to do turndown service and you didn't answer the door. She came in and you weren't here."

"I was on the roof," she says, sounding exhausted. I'm glad she's standing up for herself but it is sad that she needs to—against the man who was supposed to raise her.

"The roof," he says, looking even angrier. "You took her there."

Now I am the one exhausted. "Yes, and I can't bring myself to regret it even seeing what it did to her. She should not be locked up like this. It's killing her. Can't you see that?"

A muscle in his jaw ticks. "The only thing I see is a leech. That's what you are. You see a poor little rich girl and think it's your big payday. Well, you aren't getting a cent from her."

Of course I already have her money, but I don't want it. That's the irony of my life. Getting what I want and then wishing I had something else. "Are you any better? Wanting to marry a woman thirty years younger than you. One you've helped hide herself away."

It looks like a vein might pop out of his forehead. "She told you that?"

"I'm right here," Bea says, cross now. "And I can't believe you two are fighting over me like you're dogs and I'm a bone. I want to be alone now. I need to rest."

She does need to rest but not alone. Perhaps I can convince her to let me stay, once we are rid of this arrogant bastard with his Italian suit. I know that I can wrap her in her bubble—stifling though it is—and make her feel safe again. There are questions I should ask this Edward, confirmations to make, accusations to consider, but in the face of this unfamiliar man I'm more concerned with Bea. "I'll stay with you tonight."

And then the man gives me a look so imperious it looks exactly like it did when I was a child. "You are nothing but trash," he says, his voice the same from my memories. "That much is obvious from looking at you. Not to mention hearing you. I recognize the accent. Marrakesh?"

It's him. My heart pounds a war drum. "Tangier, actually."

"Yes, that sounds right." A smirk, which seals his fate.

And then I'm on top of him, taking him by surprise. I'm not seven years old anymore. He can't throw me off like I'm a pest to be disposed of. Can't lock me in the closet this time, not with my hands wrapped around his fucking throat. His eyes are wide, mouth open as he struggles to take in air.

"Paulette Bellmont," I say between gritted teeth. "Perhaps you remember her. She was a maid in a hotel. You stayed in the penthouse. Do you recognize my accent now?"

His mouth closes and opens, like a stupid fish. There are choking sounds.

"What are you doing?" Bea is beside me, tugging at my hands, not nearly hard enough to pull me away; *nothing* could pull me away. She looks shocked, horrified. Like I'm the monster instead of this asshole on the ground. "Let him go."

For a moment my fingers loosen. When Bea asks me to do something, I wish to do it. When she wants me, I wish to deliver. It goes beyond my regular desire to please women. Beyond any sense of professional duty. This is about Beatrix, a woman I never deserved to even touch.

Much less love. God, I love her. In the riot of emotion inside me, this much is clear.

But I have been waiting my whole life to do this.

"You followed her home one night," I say, my voice hard, my hands tight around the neck beneath me, pleading with Bea with my eyes to understand. "She did not hear you. Perhaps because the street was busy and loud, like always. Or because she was tired from working for twelve hours straight."

Bea's rose-colored lips part in surprise. "What are you talking about? You know Edward?"

"You pushed your way in the door after her. Attacked her. The only thing you did not know is that she had a child living there. A small boy. Too weak to properly defend his mother."

"No," Bea whispers, horror in her green eyes.

Only then do I look down at the man whose skin has turned mottled red. I don't want to kill him—not yet, anyway. I want him to hear this, and the dead never listen. "You locked me in the closet."

I see the memory dawn in his red-rimmed eyes. Yes, he remembers now. There may have been other maids he hurt. Other women he followed home. But he remembers the screaming boy he trapped in the closet with a wood-worn chair, its hemp cords fraying but its frame sturdy enough to hold me in.

"And then you raped her."

"She was nothing," he rasps, which is a fatal error.

Perhaps he sees that when I squeeze hard enough to take away his air. He makes a terrible sound, like the back of a car scraping against the road. His eyes roll back, and I'm looking forward to the moment he becomes silent. I did not plan to become a murderer for this, but at the moment the rage swirls around me like a firestorm. The only thing left to do is burn.

A soft crying sound prods at the edge of my consciousness. It's Beatrix, begging me to stop. "Please," she says. "Stop this. Hugo, please."

For a moment it seems that I can push aside

her pleas as easily as I did before. As easily as this *Edward* pushed me aside when I was a child, but she is not a poor little rich girl no matter what he calls her. She's a woman, strong enough to call me back from the brink of madness.

Slowly my hands loosen, but they're made of cement. It feels like cracking to pry them away from where they've hardened. When they finally release, I stumble back with the force of it.

Edward collapses on the floor, coughing and choking as he tries to breathe. As he tries to live.

Did I make a mistake? "A man like him deserves to die."

Bea kneels on the floor, her hands clasped together in futile prayer. Or maybe not so futile. She bent me to her will, after all. It makes me resent her, even while I recognize how much power she has over me. I would not change it if I could, but I hate that she wants me to let him be.

Her eyes are solemn. "A man like *you* doesn't deserve to be a killer."

Don't I? I hadn't thought I deserved anything at all. Definitely not the delicate woman who just pulled me off my mother's rapist with the force of her will alone.

"Then he gets away with it," I say, my voice dull.

It had always been coming to this, hadn't it? Mama knew. Even then she knew.

The rich can get away with anything. Even now most would consider me a rich man. I could probably hurt a poor maid in this hotel and get away with it. How sick is that? I never would, but it does not change the potential. How does it stop? How does it ever stop?

"No," Bea says, urgent. "We can tell the police. You witnessed it. We can—"

A short shake of my head. "That long ago? And my mother is dead now."

She gasps. "Did he…?"

"No," I say with a bitter laugh. "It was cancer who finished her off. But I'm not sure she ever really lived after he hurt her. She was far too busy looking over her shoulder for that."

"God." She looks at Edward like he's someone she's never seen before. "How could you?"

He has only recovered enough to get words out one at a time, coughing each one out, spitting it at her feet. "You. Believe. This. Piece. Of. Trash."

She stands up, holding herself with a remarkable poise considering only thirty minutes ago she was having an anxiety attack on the roof, curled into a ball. "I notice that's not a denial. Did you do it, Edward? Of course you did. I can see it in your face."

He snarls at her. "You. Fucked. Him."

I move to stand in front of her. She may not want my protection in this, but she's going to get it. "Don't speak to her that way. In fact don't speak to her at all. Be grateful she let you live, because she is the only reason you're able to take a breath right now. Be grateful and get the fuck out."

"You can't kick me out. I own this hotel."

"Actually," Bea says from behind me. "Your holding company owns the holding company which owns the holding company that owns this hotel. And my lease on the penthouse still stands. And I'm telling you to get out, too."

He narrows his eyes. "I can void your lease. You know that."

She takes a shuddery breath. "Then do it."

Slowly he picks himself up, looking like an old, broken man. But when he stands up straight, he stares down at us like we're trash. No, I'm the one he sees as trash. And he's right about that. "You don't want to cross me," he says to Bea. "I would have given you everything."

"No," she says softly. "You would have taken everything. That's what you do, isn't it?"

He gives me one final look—an appraisal, this look. As if considering the man who could have killed him. Weighing whether he would survive another fight. No, he wouldn't. Not even Bea could save him if he challenged me again. Nothing could save him if he hurts a single wild, copper-colored hair on her head.

Perhaps he senses that, because he turns and limps out of the room, keeping his head held high.

As soon as the elevator doors close behind him, I turn to Bea. "Are you all right?"

She holds up a hand as if I might hurt her, which makes me freeze. "I need you to go, too."

Shock is a thousand tons of bricks on my chest. They make it hard to breathe. Harder to speak. "I'm sorry, Bea. I didn't mean for that to happen in front of you."

"But you did mean for it to happen, didn't you? That's why you came last night, without me even having to pay. Not because you're interested in me, not because you're a friend. So that you could find out something about the owner of the hotel."

Shame is acid in my gut. "I care about you, Bea."

A small smile. "Is that the company line? The

official response when a client is foolish enough to think she's special to you?"

"It's not a line. I care about you more than I should, more than I imagined was possible. More than I ever cared about a woman before. *Mon Dieu*, I let him go unharmed for you."

"You only had access to him because of me," she shoots back.

There's a tear down the center of me, its edges singed with guilt. The past and present. Revenge and a woman I can't ever have. "What will you do?"

She shakes her head. "I don't know. Look for somewhere else to live, most likely. Edward probably has his lawyers looking for a loophole in the contract right now. I mean, it's not going to be hard. They wrote the contract when my trust leased the penthouse."

"I'm sorry."

"No, you didn't do anything wrong. What you said... what happened to your mother... to *you*, it's horrifying. I can't believe that he... and well, somehow I'm not as surprised as I should be. He's always thought he was above the rules."

Relief suffuses me. She understands. "I knew he might have ties to this hotel, but that's all. I did not know for sure that he was the owner. It might have been a dead end, but that isn't why I came last night. I came because I wanted to see you."

She closes her eyes and takes a deep breath. When she looks at me again, her eyes are clear. Poor little rich girl, he called her? How can he look at her, standing here like a goddess, and think she is anything but strong? "I understand why you did it. More than you know." She has a sad little laugh. "I used to dream about getting my hands on the Somali pirates who killed my parents. Not that I would have been able to… you know, choke the life out of them."

"I stopped. I stopped for you." How could that not be enough? Why doesn't she see? That was everything to me. My driving force. I gave up my past for her, for a chance at a future, and now I'm left with nothing.

Her eyes glisten with tears. "But I can't trust you. God, I barely *know* you."

"You do know me," I say, urgent. "What you said in the video… that was all true."

"You saw that?" She shakes her head, sad and lost. "I can't trust anything anymore. Not even myself. I thought Edward had my best interests at heart, even if he was a little pompous about it. But he was a monster all along. You need to go."

"What if he comes back?" What if he forces his way inside this penthouse? What if he pushes her down on the bed? Bile rises in my throat, knowing what he's capable of.

She shakes her head. "I can protect myself more than you think. More than he thinks."

"Let me stay. We don't have to do anything. We won't have sex or even talk if you're not ready for that. I'll sleep on the couch, but I'm not going to leave you alone."

"It's my decision," she says, and I can see her shutting down. I can see the walls come up around her like the marble walls of L'Etoile and the high windows. Like the private elevator that only she can use. "And if you don't listen to me, you'll be as bad as him."

Dread squeezes my heart. "I would never force you."

"Then go."

CHAPTER TWENTY-TWO

THE DEN IS quieter in early afternoon, a steady hum of conversation instead of the raucous crowd. I'm surprised to see Sutton sitting in an armchair in front of the fire, a beer dangling from its neck, the glass beaded with condensation.

I sit down in the chair next to him. "A little early," I say, nodding toward the beer.

It's an invitation for him to tell me what's wrong. He takes a swallow before answering. "Needed a break from the office."

"Problems in paradise?" I ask, my voice light. The construction and real estate company he owns with Christopher does well. And so far there hasn't been conflict between the two men. I suppose it's only a matter of time. They're both strong-willed and stubborn in their own ways.

"You could say that." Sutton leans forward and sets down the beer between his boots, studying the ground like it has the solution to life's problems. "There's this woman."

I groan. "No talk of women. Not today."

His eyebrows go up. "You love talking about women."

"Only good things. And I have no good things to say today."

He laughs. "Don't tell me Hugo Bellmont finally met his match. The virgin?"

She's not a virgin anymore, but I don't mention that. I'm sure he can fill in the blanks. I put up a finger for the cocktail waitress, because today we are drinking early. "Apparently you've met your match, too. Tell me about her."

"It's not like that. I mean, she's beautiful. Smart. Like crazy smart."

"Does she use words too big for you?"

He snorts, not bothering to argue the point. Sutton is basically a genius; he just hides it behind a Southern drawl. "That's not exactly the problem."

"Then what is it?" The waitress brings my brandy, and I take a sip.

"Christopher. She's his stepsister. Or at least they used to be. I'm a little hazy on the background except that I know there's something there."

I look into the fire so he can't see that it troubles me. There's history between Christopher and this Harper. And if it comes between them, it will disrupt more than the company. It will disrupt the Thieves Club, a friendship I've come to enjoy greatly. "History is in the past, my friend. So what are you going to do about this?"

"The only thing I can do. The only thing I've ever done."

The answer is simple for a man as hard and ambitious as Sutton. "Go after her."

He nods. "I would prefer that it didn't interfere with business."

"I would have preferred that also, but here we are drinking at three in the afternoon."

We lapse into a contemplative silence. I didn't come here expecting to see anyone I knew. Sutton knows better than to push me when I don't want to talk. It doesn't happen often, but when it does, it usually has to do with Melissande. And history. But history is in the past, as I said.

So what am I going to do about it?

The moments that follow are a brief reprieve, but in the back of my mind I know what I have to do. Revenge has been the thing that drove me for years. Now it will be something else, but no matter what I choose to do, I'll be left alone. That's all I deserve, really.

The waitress returns, this time with a note on

her tray. *Hugo Bellmont*, it says on the front.

And inside: *Come upstairs. – D*

"I have been summoned," I say to Sutton, dropping the note on the small oak table between us.

He reads it with surprise. "What's your business with him? Do you need backup?"

It does feel good to have friends who would have my back, but he has his own problems. Problems of the female persuasion. And I need to solve this one myself. Need to solve it alone.

At the bottom of the stairs I pass by Penny, who is Damon's girl. I recognize her from around the Den and from our one meeting at Beau Ciel. "Good afternoon," I tell her with a small bow.

Her cheeks turn a little pink. It used to bring me pleasure that I could make any woman—even ones contented in their relationships—blush, but instead there's only emptiness. "Damon's waiting for you," she says, revealing that she knows more about his business than some people would suspect.

"*Merci.* And do you have any words of advice for me? He has quite a reputation."

"Don't believe a word they say. I mean, some of it's real, but you'll never really know which parts."

"Very reassuring," I say drily. "You are a good match for him, to be sure."

She laughs. "He's a softie inside."

I'm still shaking my head, a small smile on my face, when I reach the top of the stairs. It is only such a ridiculous statement as Damon Scott being a softie that could make me laugh. It occurs to me that perhaps that's Penny's goal, to cheer me up against all odds. In which case she truly *is* a good match for the man who sits at a desk set far back in a dark room.

He does not look up when I enter, but I know he hears me. There's nothing that happens in the Den that he doesn't know about. Maybe even in the whole of Tanglewood.

"Good afternoon," I say, neutral. "You asked for me?"

Of course he did not *ask*. It was a command. I do not take offense, not if he delivers what I need him to do. He looks up and sets his pen down. "Our deal. Do you still want it?"

I step farther into the room but don't bother to sit, not even when he inclines his head at the oversize leather chairs in front of the desk. This isn't a deal I want to sit for. "Melissande. You want her ruined. You haven't told me why, and I don't imagine you will. But I agree to that."

"And in return I will ruin Edward Marchand. The owner of L'Etoile."

This is what it feels like to be torn in half, the halves pulled away completely. I'm two pieces now, the one from the past and the one adrift. "No."

One eyebrow rises. "No?"

Well, that's something at the least. I have managed to surprise Damon Scott. "Instead I wish for you to purchase the hotel for me. I will provide the money, but the owner may take some persuasion."

Damon leans back, pondering. "I have some knowledge of your portfolio. It's significant. Probably enough, but only barely. You won't have anything left."

And with Melissande ruined, I won't be able to work in this town. At least not for the prices I normally command. She will do her best to blackball me and probably succeed.

It does not matter. I don't matter, not if it means Bea can be safe.

"Do we have a deal?" I ask, my voice even.

"Consider it done."

I set down a flash drive on his desk. It contains photographs I took in her office late last night of her ledger, written in her own handwriting. Names and dates and dollar amounts. The fact that she's a madam is well-known in the underworld of the city. No cop would make a move on her for selling sex. Half of them are under her payroll. And the other half… well, she would be out within twenty-four hours and make it her mission to destroy them.

That's why I've circled the names of boys and girls I know to be under eighteen. It's a dark truth of the sex industry that this happens. When they don't have a good family, when the system fails them, it's the only way they survive. There are clients who prefer the young ones.

Which is one of the reasons Melissande wanted me all those years ago. She probably enjoyed that I worshipped her at the beginning, as well. But it wasn't long before she put me to work.

Damon nods. "A pleasure doing business with you."

No, I have experience with pleasure. This was something else. "You'll let me know?"

"It will take a couple days. I'll be in touch."

And this is how you make a deal with the devil. By selling the most valuable thing I have for the only person worth anything to me. Losing L'Etoile will be nothing to a man like Edward Marchand. It will not ruin him, not when he has a hundred other more valuable properties. Decades of searching for revenge, only to give it up in a single afternoon.

But it will mean freedom for Bea, which is the most important thing now. The only thing. I traded everything for her to feel safe, for her to never again tremble in fear.

CHAPTER TWENTY-THREE

I HAVE AN entire bottle of brandy sitting on the counter.

And beside it is a stack of papers that constitutes the signed and executed contract rendering me the new owner of L'Etoile. When Mama worked as a maid, I looked at the hotel with awe, with anger, with distrust—but I never imagined I would own a place like it.

Now I am the proprietor.

Well, I won't become too comfortable with the title. I will have to face Bea soon so that we can transfer the title to her name. It won't matter if I promise never to evict her or coerce her into anything. Only when she owns her suite free and clear will she truly feel safe.

Not tonight, however. Tonight I plan to get very drunk. After spending all day at a lawyer's office, signing away almost every last cent I own, it seems the only fitting thing to do. At least I did not have to see Edward there. He signed the night before. Putting up quite a protest, Damon said, but in the end the Scott name held enough clout—and enough fear—in the city to convince him to sign. And Edward ended up fairly compensated for the hotel, something that I cannot help but dwell on tonight, with my bank account and investments depleted.

I reach for a glass as the door buzzes. Is it Melissande? I haven't heard from her, but I imagine that won't last. She will have some words for me once she realizes what I've done. Unless Damon makes it hard enough for her that she has to leave Tanglewood.

My phone is open to Bea Sharp's page, where nothing new has been uploaded for a week. Her longest break, except for the one time she had the flu, one of the comments says—but even then she posted an update to let everyone know. The fans are in a frenzy about the absence, worried and dramatic, but none of it compares to the intensity of my own guilt.

I felt bad for making her cry the first night, but this is worse. I hurt her. Not her beautiful body but the tender heart inside. No wonder she kicked me out.

My finger flicks across the screen, and the security app appears. I stare at the photo a long second, trying to blink away the mirage. It's dark outside, but the light clearly illuminates her upturned nose, her green eyes. Her copper curls. "Bea," I breathe.

She's here. Why is she here? *How* is she here?

I press the button to buzz her in the main door downstairs, but I don't wait for her to climb the stairs to my loft. Instead I'm out the door and running down to meet her, my heart pounding louder than my footfalls, hope a wild and unmistakable beat. I catch her up in my arms as she falls, trembling, afraid. "What are you doing?" I demand, my throat tight with fear for her. Not that she would be in danger in the world, but she will *feel* as though she is. Her body will undergo the same stress, the same reactions as if she were kidnapped by Somali pirates even if nothing happens.

"I took a cab," she whispers, her voice shaking.

"*Mon Dieu.*" I don't wait for her to give me permission this time. I lift her and carry her up the stairs, my stride fast and steady. Once we're inside the loft, I shut the door and think about where to put her. Nothing about this place is what she's used to. Sleek modern furniture instead of embellished antiques. Crisp leather instead of thick brocade.

The bed, I realize. The white sheets on my bed aren't trimmed with lace, but they're close enough. No other woman has ever spent the night with me in the bed, but it feels completely natural that Bea would be there. I stride into the bedroom and set her down gently, pushing the hair back from her face. "Why did you do it, Bea?"

"I had to see you." Her lower lip trembles, and I'm terribly afraid she's going to cry.

"You could have called me. I would have come."

"No," she says, a little too loud. This is when I realize that she is more than afraid. She's perhaps tipsy. "I have to apologize to you. God, you had just seen the man who… And then I told you to leave."

She's definitely crying now, tears thick in her throat, fat drops on her copper lashes.

"You are killing me," I tell her honestly. "Don't cry."

Her lip trembles while she makes a valiant effort to stop. It isn't quite enough. "I couldn't stop thinking about your face when I asked you to go. And after everything you'd done. The picnic. You wanted me to get out of there, and I should have, a long time ago, and now I have to leave—"

"Shhh." I consider telling her about the sale of L'Etoile. I could show her the contract in the next room, but that will only raise questions of why Edward had been willing to part with it. The important thing is that she calm down now. I'll tell her about the hotel later. "Don't worry about that. Everything will work out. I promise, Bea."

"It's fine," she says, quite loud, and I realize she's more than tipsy. She's completely wasted. "I did it. Look! I'm outside the hotel right now, and I'm not freaking out."

Except that she had to get drunk before she could come. And what happens when she sobers up? I'm afraid we're in for an even worse panic attack than before. "You amaze me," I tell her gently. "This is a beautiful first step. But right now I want you to go back with me."

She looks crestfallen. "Why?"

"Because I don't have a piano, and I want to hear you play." As I say the words, I discover that they're true. This loft doesn't suit her. It's an impersonal husk, rather like myself. Even if she is able to leave L'Etoile on a regular basis, that penthouse is her home. And, when she plays music, her soul.

She starts to cry again. "I do want to play. I do."

"And you will," I tell her. "Very soon."

"No." Her green eyes are deep, reflective pools. "I haven't played since you left. How crazy is that? For years it was almost the only way I could speak. And then nothing."

I don't think it has anything to do with my absence. More likely she's terrified of being forced from her home after the confrontation with Edward. "You remember my Bugatti?"

She shakes her head, eyes wide. "Noooo."

Oh, she is an adorable drunk. I would enjoy the experience more if I didn't know how little time with her I have left. "You watched me arrive the first night," I remind her. "It's very pretty. Not as pretty as you, but still. Shall we take it back to L'Etoile?"

"Okay," she says. "I'll try not to throw up. The cab driver was not happy."

I decide to bring both the contract and the bottle of brandy with me. Something tells me I might need both of them before I'm done.

Chapter Twenty-Four

THE NEXT MORNING I wake up with a massive hangover and a pair of yellow eyes staring down at me. It takes me a moment to make the world stop spinning and orient myself.

Where the hell am I? The penthouse of L'Etoile.

What *is* that? Ah, that's right. The cat.

My voice comes out scratchy and thick. "*Bonjour*, Minette."

She's apparently warmed up enough that she's cuddling on my chest. Either that or she was plotting ways to kill me in my sleep. Gingerly I move the kitty aside and wander out of the bedroom.

A room service tray sits on the small table, filled with pastries and an omelet. I must have been sleeping very hard not to notice it arrive. And from behind the closed door I hear music playing. I believe the song is "Breakaway" by Kelly Clarkson, though it's been changed enough that

I'm not sure. It's softer now, almost haunting.

Feeling like an intruder, I knock softly and step inside.

Bea sits at the bench looking impossibly fresh. Her hair is still dark and damp from the shower. I probably could have slept through an earthquake. Only vaguely do I remember working my way through the bottle of brandy while Bea played the piano beside me. There is an even hazier memory of singing "Hotel California" as a duet.

We were both drunk, and now we're both hungover.

Though Bea's smile is too bright and too genuine. "Are you hungry?" she asks.

So apparently I'm the only one hungover. "No, thank you. Is it all right if I shower?"

"Of course. You don't have to ask me that."

Actually I do, because you'll soon be the new owner of this hotel.

That's what I should say to her, but I can't quite bring myself to do it. Because I know that the sooner I say that, the sooner this ends. And she looks so lovely in a silk and lace robe. So lovely in her casual majesty. It makes me want to fall to my knees, to beg her to stay. But anything other than leaving would be a way to tie her down, to make her owe me. I need to give her the hotel outright, without any strings attached or demands. And then I need to leave.

I won't do to her what Edward did.

"I'll be back in a few minutes," I say roughly, because I need a cold shower and approximately ten thousand gallons of coffee before I'm ready to have that conversation.

In the bathroom I find a drawer with a couple unused toothbrushes wrapped in clear plastic, the kind the hotel probably sends up to forgetful travelers. I feel much better after I brush my teeth, but I need a shower. In the end I'm not quite self-flagellant enough to make the water cold. I make it hot instead, standing under the spray and letting it pound away some of the tension.

A sound catches my attention, and then a gust of cool air as the shower door opens.

Bea stands on the marble tile, looking shy and knowing at once in a gold silk robe. A virgin. A siren. I'm not sure my mind will ever wrap itself around her. I'm not sure I'd ever want to. I crave both parts of her, *all* of her.

"Can I come in?" she asks.

Already my body reacts to her, hardening, turning hot and eager. "There's nothing I want more, Bea. But I don't know if I can be gentle right now."

She tugs on the silk holding her robe together, revealing the glory of her body—pale skin and dusky nipples, high breasts with freckles across the slopes of them. Her belly narrows and then flares out again to hips I long to hold as I pound into her.

Between her legs her hair is a darker color, almost bronze. My cock throbs just looking at her.

The silk pools behind her, and she steps into the shower with me. "Then be rough."

It's been so long since I've had sex for only myself. Have I ever done that?

Have I ever touched a woman's breasts only to feel them in my hands? Have I ever sucked her nipples because I love the feel of her? Have I ever slid my fingers through her slit, blunt and greedy, because I needed to feel where my cock would be? It is a revelation to do it now. A miracle.

Bea gasps and arches, giving me better access to her pussy. "Whatever you want."

"Yes," I mutter, letting the need overtake me. For the first time. This is how she felt that night, being a virgin. It's the way I feel right now, doing this with her. I push two fingers inside her, slick from her arousal and the hot spray of the shower. "I want this."

She moans, leaning back against the tile. "Yes."

"I should prepare you more," I warn her. "You will feel this later."

"Make yourself feel good," she whispers, her eyes an unfathomable sea. She has depths I've never explored. Depths I never *will* explore, because I won't be here that long.

I'm here now, so I make it count, lifting her up against the tile wall, spreading her thighs wide, and notching my cock against her. My voice comes out as a growl. "Say it again."

Her head falls back, exposing her throat. "Whatever you want."

I thrust home, clenching my teeth against the ecstasy of her. She pulses around me, and it feels so good I want to make her do it again. "That's right," I say, my lids heavy. "Touch yourself, Bea. Come around my cock. I want to feel you."

She reaches down, whimpering as she finds her clit. It's too direct, I think. A little too harsh, touching herself while she's spread open and sensitive, but I don't tell her to stop. It feels too good when her pussy grasps my cock like a fist. "Oh my God," she whispers.

Whatever you want. The words swirl around me in the hot steam, and for the first time I'm free. "Bite me," I gasp, because that's something I would not have asked for. I want it now.

She turns her head, making a delicate bite on my arm where I support us against the tile. Her hand moves faster on her clit, and I know she's close. Close, but I want more. Always more.

"Harder," I say, my teeth gritted.

She comes with a keening cry, biting down hard enough I see stars. I ride out her climax while her pussy squeezes my cock, and then I lose myself in her. I thrust into her, relentless and burning hot, turning her climax into a second and a third, until they string together in an endless litany, her voice echoing off the tile, her body wet and welcoming around mine.

I take her again and again, long after I should let her rest, only because I want to. *Whatever you want*, she says, so I pretend we have forever.

Chapter Twenty-Five

WE SPEND THE rest of the day making love. I have had plenty of sex in my life—the passionate kind, the animalistic kind. The paid kind. There has been sex in my life but never love.

Which is why I force myself to leave the bed while she sleeps, to dress quietly, to write a note explaining that the deed will be hers. For such a large property it will require a visit to the lawyer to finalize the transfer, but I make it clear—it will be hers, outright. She owes me nothing. In fact, she most likely won't ever see me again.

Perhaps I could have been gone. I should have been.

Instead I find myself digging through the pantry for a can of tuna. I open it for the cat, who gobbles it almost faster than seems healthy, swallowing whole chunks of fish.

"Where are you going?" Bea stands in the doorway from the bedroom, holding the lace-trimmed sheet around herself like a toga. I suppose she could look nothing less than glorious, her body well used, her hair even wilder than ever before.

"Home," I say, though the word is rather generous considering the emptiness of the loft.

She moves farther into the living area. "Oh."

"It's for the best," I say, managing a small smile for her. "I wrote out the details here, but you will be able to stay at L'Etoile. I made sure of that."

Her brow furrows. "What do you mean?"

It's only here that I realize the note was an act of cowardice. This woman has the strength to confront her worst fears. I can find some to tell her it won't be as bad as that. "I hope you continue to push your boundaries. To visit the rooftop garden or other places in Tanglewood. There are pianos all around the city for you. But you won't be forced to leave."

"You talked to Edward," she says, speaking cautiously because I'm sure she knows that if I confronted him a second time, there would be no talking.

"I had a third party do it for me. He was convinced it would be in his best interest to sell the hotel. Which means you're free. You don't have to leave, except on your own terms."

A sense of peace flows out from her. "You did that for me?"

"I would do anything for you." Even leave.

Her gaze turns to the stack of papers. "Is that from Edward, then?"

"In a manner of speaking. Actually I purchased the property from him, because I had to make sure he would go through with it. I'll transfer the deed into your name as soon as the lawyer can arrange it. Then it will be yours."

"You mean I'm going to buy it from you?"

"No, Bea. It's a gift. There are no strings attached."

Her mouth drops open. "I could never accept a gift that big."

It has to be this way. For her, so she is never coerced into anything she doesn't want, never fearful of it. And for me, because I don't know how to offer anything but this. "It's already yours in all but name, Bea. The title is only to make sure you're safe."

She takes a step closer, standing right in front of me now. "I'm already safe. If you own L'Etoile, then I'm safe here, with you."

I'm moved that she has such confidence in me. "I never want you to doubt it."

"I'll take the hotel from you if that's what you

want. I would be happy to do that. The building may be old and kind of, you know, gaudy, but I love it. And I love the people here."

"Good."

"But it will be a purchase. Not a gift."

I open my mouth to object, but to be fair, the woman probably has more money than God. Then why does it make me feel like I'm crawling out of my skin to accept? Like I'm losing far more than the woman I care about. "*Non.*"

"*Oui,*" she says, implacable.

I'm not above pleading, at least not with her. "Bea, you must understand how much I've come to care about you. It's not like the other women. They aren't even—"

For maybe the first time since I moved here, I struggle for words.

She smiles a little. "I know."

That makes me pause. "You know?"

"You make your own kind of music. Not with your fingers on the keys. With your whole body. I thought I was just imagining it. After all, what did I know? I was a virgin. I don't know how it usually is between a man and a woman. But I know about music. You can't fake that kind of passion."

I breathe out in relief, that she understands

what I could not find the words to say. There is too much in my past to love easily or lightly; the grooves run too deep. I speak with my body instead, and in that language Bea is an unexpected prodigy.

I give her a small bow. "In that case I accept your terms. You will buy the hotel."

"And I hope you will come visit me here."

My throat becomes tight. I would give almost anything to be with Bea, but I'm not sure I could handle being paid for the honor. Not anymore. "In a professional capacity?"

"If that's the only way I can have you, yes." She swallows hard. "But I'm going to be honest with you, even though it terrifies me. It terrifies me more than taking a cab to your loft, which was a lot. I want more than that. I want everything."

"Everything?" It seems impossible that I could have this. For so long I lived only for revenge. And for pleasure. I thought that would be enough until I met Bea.

She made me realize I want more than that. "What you said in the shower," I say, gruff.

Her lips twist into a secret feminine smile, and for the first time in my life I feel my skin flush hot. Am I blushing? *Mon Dieu.* She really has ruined me for anyone else. "I think I asked you to be rough with me."

"Something else," I say, though I'm danger-ously close to being rough with her on the dining table. There is only one thing I want more than sex with her right now.

"That you should make yourself feel good," she says, letting the sheet fall away from her body.

"Minx," I say on a groan. "Witch. Siren. You said something else to me."

"Whatever you want," she whispers.

And then I take her in my arms. "Everything. *Mon Dieu*, I want everything with you."

She wraps her arms around my neck and gives me all of that and more. The fire in her wild hair, the freckles scattered across her body. The acceptance in her beautiful moss eyes. There is a whole universe waiting for us, and we find it one star at a time.

Chapter Twenty-Six

THE NIGHT SKY stretches to infinity, but the moment is almost unbearably intimate. We are lying on the rooftop, naked but for a lace-edged sheet we stole from her bed. Bea's body is slung over mine, her hair a pleasant cloud of sensation against my neck. Her hand plays idly over my chest, tugging lightly at the springy hair, tracing down the muscles of my abs.

"Are you sad?" she asks. "About Edward?"

"He lost his hold on you. That's enough." It's more than whatever wealth he has in the world, actually. More precious than gold. Though nothing will ever be punishment enough for what he did to my mother. So I suppose it's fitting he gave up something priceless. "The truth is I feel more guilty than anything."

"About Melissande. Has she called you again?"

"No." I stare at the sky, which feels heavier when I think about her. "Not since I gave her a few thousand to start over somewhere else."

"What she did was wrong, Hugo. Selling children. You were a child, too, when she took advantage of you. She didn't deserve your loyalty."

"Loyalty is a strange thing. It doesn't always need an excuse. In the case of Melissande, she took me from a place where I had no future and turned me into something women paid thousands of dollars to spend time with."

Anger flashes through Bea's green eyes, which are usually so calm. "She has no idea what you're worth. She never did."

Bemusement is a warm fire in my chest. "You are kind, *mon amie*."

"Yes, that's me. Kind and so incredibly selfless that I'm willing to spend my nights with the most sought-after man in Tanglewood, that I'm willing to have this body—" She walks her fingers down my abdomen. My cock is a predictable creature. It becomes hard beneath the sheet, despite the number of times I've taken her this night. "—bring me pleasure."

A small laugh. "If there's one thing I've taught you, it's to appreciate pleasure."

"You taught me more than that," she says suggestively, and I know she's thinking of the rather athletic round of sex we had after our picnic of grapes and manchego.

I touch my finger to the bronze of her eyebrows, tracing them. "While you have learned your lessons well, there is still plenty more to teach."

"Oh?" she asks, her lips forming a perfect peach circle.

"I expect we will spend many nights on the rooftop."

She laughs. "I thought you were the one who wanted me to leave the hotel."

"*Oui*, but you have taught me things as well. For example, you taught me to appreciate staying between these four walls." It has been three days since I signed over L'Etoile to her. Since that time I have not left. There has been only sex and talking and the occasional break for delicious food. "Perhaps we will leave next week. Where would you like to go?'

She draws swirling circles on my skin. "There is an exhibit at the Tanglewood Art Museum I've had my eye on."

I think of the traveling exhibits. "The one with mummies?"

"No."

"The one about bugs in gemstones."

"No."

And then I groan. "It's the instruments of the Middle Ages, isn't it? That's a permanent exhibit, *mon amie*. Part of the original collection, I believe. It hurts my heart that you have not seen it."

"I know," she says, hiding her face against my chest.

"We will work up to it," I promise.

Naturally I don't mention that I know the director of the museum on an intimate level, that she was a regular client who was rather peeved when I told her I would no longer be working. Perhaps I could even arrange a private show of the instruments for Bea...if I made it worth the director's time. But no, we will attend the museum the old-fashioned way, with a ticket of admissions.

She shivers in my arms, still not quite ready to venture out. "Okay."

"I must tell you one of the most wonderful things about leaving your bed. It's thinking of all the delicious things to do to you when I return."

Her hand slips under the blanket. "Delicious?"

My breath catches when she touches somewhere particularly sensitive. "Yes."

My innocent ex-virgin has turned into a sex

goddess. Her fist closes around my cock while her lips hover near my ear. "I do love the way you taste," she whispers.

I groan and press my hips up toward the night. "Please."

She moves down my body and takes me to heaven with her mouth, her hands. Her eyes, full of reckless confidence. This is how I want her—unafraid. The climax hits me, almost violent in its strength, making me choke out her name in a litany, "Bea, Bea, Bea."

It feels incredible, but nowhere near as good as it does to flip her onto her back. To turn the sly grin into an O of shocked bliss. We dine on the best food available in the city, in the world, but none of the flavors compare to the sweet salt of her arousal. The essence of this woman, which has become like sustenance. The taste that made me come awake, after so long spent in the dark.

EPILOGUE

Six months later

I SPENT MANY evenings at the Den before I met Bea, but none of them were a Saturday night.

Those were reserved for work.

Now I'm no longer a male escort. I suppose you could say I'm an investor now, though that word is rather boring. My modest fortune was restored when Bea purchased L'Etoile from me, and so I'm free to play with money like the Monopoly game. Though I consider my true profession to be pleasing Bea. That's something I find far more satisfying.

At first I thought we would focus on the museum, but then I realized another place would hold a far greater intellectual curiosity for her with its ever-changing population, its unique cross section of the city. The Den. It also had a built-in support system. And so we visited a month after I moved into the penthouse, leaving quickly before she could succumb to panic.

And then we went again. And again.

The members of the Thieves Club were fascinated to meet the woman who had tied me down, but it was Penny who accepted Bea into her fold. For her part Bea has flourished among a new group of people, like a flower that has survived in brittle, almost desertlike conditions, which has finally been given water.

I'm standing behind the curtain on the small stage set up in the ballroom. The Bluthner grand piano has been restored by craftsmen and expertly tuned, ready for Bea to play for the small crowd of the city's elite.

If she doesn't hyperventilate first.

She leans over a potted plant, heaving like she might throw up. It would be a waste of the beautiful roasted lamb I prepared for her, and it would not taste nearly as good on the way back up.

"*Mon amie,*" I say softly, a little coaxing. "Come here."

She moans her refusal. "I can't do this. Why did I think I could do this?"

"Because you can do anything. This small show is only one small thing in a very large list."

"There's a *stage,*" she says. "I've never been on a stage before."

"You have played for millions of viewers instead. You will do very well up there. And I'll be waiting in the eaves for you to return, to congratulate you." My tone makes it clear this congratulation would take a sexy form.

"Can we do that now?" she asks, hopeful.

Always ready, this one.

"But no, they are about to begin." I glance between the two heavy velvet curtains at the chairs filled with men in tuxes and women in glittering gowns. "Did you know that there was once a virginity auction on this very stage?"

"What?" Bea looks scandalized—and also curious, which I had hoped for.

"Yes, and now she returns as a guest." Tickets to this event were extremely sought after. The debut of the Internet phenomenon Bea Sharp. "There she is on the front row. Next to Harper."

Avery James looks beautiful and composed, though the growling animal of a man beside her probably has something to do with it. No one in attendance would dare make even the smallest remark to shame her. Gabriel Miller would rip their head off.

"You know her?" Bea narrows her eyes. "Did *you* attend the auction?"

"Of course not. It was a Saturday."

She laughs softly, shaking her head. "Well done. You've successfully distracted me. Now all I can do is picture those two having sex."

"Very beautiful people, those two. I'm sure they are pleasant pictures. However, they're nothing compared to what you and I will look like after your show."

The corner of her lips turns up. "What will we look like?"

"This will be new. And impossible to describe. Much better if I show you."

She looks skeptical. "Something new?"

Our nights have been passionate and inventive. I have many tricks up my sleeve. That has less to do with my previous profession. It's Bea herself. Her body, her smile. Her music. She makes me dream up new ways to make love to her every night.

"Something new," I repeat, pointing to the curtains where Damon Scott appears.

"Is the star ready to go on?" he says, but it's not really a question. I don't think he would look very kindly on her if he had to refund all of these people's money. So it's a good thing I don't doubt her.

Bea takes a deep breath and nods. "Let's do this."

I stand with her in silence, my arms around her, my lips against her temple, while Damon gives a stirring and awe-inspiring introduction. It includes her video-watched stats and the incredible artists who have praised her work. He finishes with, "Please welcome the luminous Bea Sharp to the Den tonight."

It's only with reluctance that I let her go, because she deserves to shine.

She deserves it as much as I deserve to witness it.

Her green eyes look back at me, filled with serenity that I knew would be there. When it comes to music there is nothing that makes this woman nervous. Not even the Den, which she has managed to visit a few times now. Not even this crowd of wealthy and powerful people, all of them watching her with wonder. There is only grace and confidence as she crosses the small stage and sits down on the bench.

Beyond the raised frame of the piano, I see Harper send a small wave to Bea. Behind her sits Sutton, a grave expression on his face. He hides it well, but it's clear how he feels about the vibrant young woman. Even less clear is how Christopher feels, though he does not seem to be in attendance tonight. There is sexual attraction, to be sure.

Inappropriate between siblings, even if the connection was made through marriage and not biology. It remains to be seen whether there is anything more.

Bea takes a breath that I recognize from the countless times I've watched her play. Her fingers find the keys without her having to look down. This instrument may be new to her, but she knows the notes like they're parts of her soul. Like they're written on her skin.

And when she plays, the stars themselves come alight.

THE END

THANK YOU!

Thank you so much for reading Hugo and Bea's story!

Don't miss the brand new romance also about a heroine who loves music...

Liam North got custody of the violin prodigy six years ago. She's all grown up now, but he still treats her like a child. No matter how much he wants her.

"Swoon-worthy, forbidden, and sexy, Liam North is my new obsession."

– New York Times bestselling author Claire Contreras

"Overture is a beautiful composition of forbidden love and undeniable desire. Skye has crafted a gripping, sensual, and intense story that left me breathless"

– USA Today bestselling author Nikki Sloane

And if you want to read more about Harper and Sutton and Christopher, you'll love SURVIVAL OF THE RICHEST. Find out what happens in this scorching love triangle!

Two billionaires determined to claim her.

And a war fought on the most dangerous battlefield—the heart.

My story starts with a plunge into the cold water of Manhattan's harbor. A strong hand hauls me back onto the deck of the luxury yacht. Christopher was supposed to be my enemy. Instead he protects me with fierce determination.

That should have been my happily ever after, but then Sutton appeared–ruthless and seductive. He doesn't care that my heart belongs to someone else, because he's determined to win. No matter the cost.

It's an impossible choice, but I can't have them both.

Sign up for the VIP Reader List to find out when I have a new book release:

www.skyewarren.com/newsletter

If you enjoyed ESCORT, you'll love the sexy virgin auction novel THE PAWN, available now!

Join my Facebook group, Skye Warren's Dark Room, for exclusive giveaways and sneak peeks of future books. Turn the page for an excerpt from Overture...

EXCERPT FROM OVERTURE

R *EST,* LIAM TOLD me.

He's right about a lot of things. Maybe he's right about this. I climb onto the cool pink sheets, hoping that a nap will suddenly make me content with this quiet little life.

Even though I know it won't.

Besides, I'm too wired to actually sleep. The white lace coverlet is both delicate and comfy. It's actually what I would have picked out for myself, except I didn't pick it out. I've been incapable of picking anything, of choosing anything, of deciding anything as part of some deep-seated fear that I'll be abandoned.

The coverlet, like everything else in my life, simply appeared.

And the person responsible for its appearance? Liam North.

I climb under the blanket and stare at the ceiling. My body feels overly warm, but it still feels good to be tucked into the blankets. The blankets *he* picked out for me.

It's really so wrong to think of him in a sexual way. He's my guardian, literally. Legally. And he has never done anything to make me think he sees *me* in a sexual way.

This is it. This is the answer.

I don't need to go skinny dipping in the lake down the hill. Thinking about Liam North in a sexual way is my fast car. My parachute out of a plane.

My eyes squeeze shut.

That's all it takes to see Liam's stern expression, those fathomless green eyes and the glint of dark blond whiskers that are always there by late afternoon. And then there's the way he touched me. My forehead, sure, but it's more than he's done before. That broad palm on my sensitive skin.

My thighs press together. They want something between them, and I give them a pillow. Even the way I masturbate is small and timid, never making a sound, barely moving at all, but I can't change it now. I can't moan or throw back my head even for the sake of rebellion.

But I can push my hips against the pillow, rocking my whole body as I imagine Liam doing more than touching my forehead. He would trail his hand down my cheek, my neck, my shoulder.

Repressed. I'm so repressed it's hard to imagine more than that.

I make myself do it, make myself trail my hand down between my breasts, where it's warm and velvety soft, where I imagine Liam would know exactly how to touch me.

You're so beautiful, he would say. *Your breasts are perfect.*

Because Imaginary Liam wouldn't care about big breasts. He would like them small and soft with pale nipples. That would be the absolute perfect pair of breasts for him.

And he would probably do something obscene and rude. Like lick them.

My hips press against the pillow, almost pushing it down to the mattress, rocking and rocking. There's not anything sexy or graceful about what I'm doing. It's pure instinct. Pure need.

The beginning of a climax wraps itself around me. Claws sink into my skin. There's almost certain death, and I'm fighting, fighting, fighting for it with the pillow clenched hard.

"Oh fuck."

The words come soft enough someone else might not hear them. They're more exhalation of breath, the consonants a faint break in the sound.

I have excellent hearing. Ridiculous, crazy good hearing that had me tuning instruments before I could ride a bike.

My eyes snap open, and there's Liam, standing there, frozen. Those green eyes locked on mine. His body clenched tight only three feet away from me. He doesn't come closer, but he doesn't leave.

Orgasm breaks me apart, and I cry out in surprise and denial and relief. "*Liam.*"

It goes on and on, the terrible pleasure of it. The wrenching embarrassment of coming while looking into the eyes of the man who raised me for the past six years.

Want to read more? Overture is available on Amazon, iBooks, Barnes & Noble, and other book retailers!

BOOKS BY SKYE WARREN

Endgame trilogy & Masterpiece Duet

The Pawn

The Knight

The Castle

The King

The Queen

Trust Fund Duet

Survival of the Richest

The Evolution of Man

Underground series

Rough

Hard

Fierce

Wild

Dirty

Secret

Sweet

Deep

Stripped series

Tough Love

Love the Way You Lie

Better When It Hurts

Even Better

Pretty When You Cry

Caught for Christmas

Hold You Against Me

To the Ends of the Earth

Standalone Books

Wanderlust

On the Way Home

Beauty and the Beast

Anti Hero

Escort

**For a complete listing of Skye Warren books,
visit
www.skyewarren.com/books**

About the Author

Skye Warren is the New York Times bestselling author of dangerous romance such as the Endgame trilogy. Her books have been featured in Jezebel, Buzzfeed, USA Today Happily Ever After, Glamour, and Elle Magazine. She makes her home in Texas with her loving family, sweet dogs, and evil cat.

Sign up for Skye's newsletter:
www.skyewarren.com/newsletter

Like Skye Warren on Facebook:
facebook.com/skyewarren

Join Skye Warren's Dark Room reader group:
skyewarren.com/darkroom

Follow Skye Warren on Instagram:
instagram.com/skyewarrenbooks

Visit Skye's website for her current booklist:
www.skyewarren.com

COPYRIGHT

This is a work of fiction. Any resemblance to actual persons, living or dead, business establishments, events or locales is entirely coincidental. All rights reserved. Except for use in a review, the reproduction or use of this work in any part is forbidden without the express written permission of the author.